BILL MANHIRE was born in Invercargill in 1946. His parents were publicans, and he grew up in small hotels in Otago and Southland. He was educated at the University of Otago and University College London, where he studied the Old Norse Sagas.

He has published a choose-your-own adventure novel, *The Brain of Katherine Mansfield*, and a critical study of the novelist Maurice Gee. Several of the stories in this collection have won prizes, but Manhire is best known for his poetry, including the award-winning *Zoetropes: Poems 1972-82*. Twice a winner of the New Zealand Book Award for poetry, he has also held a Nuffield Travelling Fellowship, and in 1989 was awarded the Arts Council's Scholarship in Letters.

Bill Manhire lives in Wellington with his wife and two children. He is Reader in English at Victoria University.

The New Land

A Picture Book

BILL MANHIRE

PACIFIC WRITERS SERIES

Published by Heinemann Reed,
a division of Octopus Publishing Group (NZ) Ltd,
39 Rawene Road, Birkenhead, Auckland.
Associated companies, branches and representatives
throughout the world.

ISBN 0 7900 0107 1

©1990, Bill Manhire
First published 1990
Printed in Australia

Acknowledgements are made to the editors of the following
magazines where some of these stories have previously
appeared: *Chelsea* (USA), *Islands* (NZ), *London Magazine* (UK),
Meanjin (Australia), *PN Review* (UK), *Span* (Australia), *Sport*
(NZ) and *Untold* (NZ). Several stories have been produced and
broadcast, some in dramatic adaptations, by Radio New
Zealand.

For bonny Maisie Aitken

CONTENTS

HIGHLIGHTS

THEY ARE IN Rotorua, but the Bellevue no longer has a view and is also double-booked. The apologetic girl at the desk is professionally reassuring. He leaves his mother in the car and hovers in the lobby while she phones around. Out on Fenton Street motels push and jostle for room. Belaire, Boulevard, Matador, Sulphur City, Rob Roy, Pineland, Ascot, Forest Court, Nikau Lodge . . . It will be all right.

Each time she puts the phone down the girl looks across and smiles to indicate she will try again. Eventually she beckons him over and asks would he like her to try one of the big hotels. Her friend at the Kiwi Panorama has reminded her about the August school holiday family packages. It might even be cheaper than a motel. As long as you eat out, she adds.

They can have three nights at the Randwick International (room rate $75), but no more because of the incoming police convention.

'It's enough, though, isn't it,' says his mother through the car window. She looks tired yet determined, she talks between bites of a tomato sandwich. 'Let's have the nights they can give us. We'll just do the main things, and then you take me home, Robert.'

He steps out on to their room's small balcony. The imitation Spanish railing curls up to hip-level. He blinks in the pale mid-afternoon sunshine. Which way is the lake? Across the road is what looks like an abandoned motel complex — a long, low, L-shaped structure made of pink and green tinted concrete blocks. The roadside windows are boarded up, there are crates of empty bottles stacked outside. A man squats on the roof, painting it a gunmetal grey.

He turns back inside where his mother sits on the huge bed

among colour brochures. He looks inside the fridge unit, which is well stocked with expensive juices and miniatures.

'I want to do the highlights, Robert. Two things tomorrow and something on Thursday.'

'It's your treat,' he says. 'Your birthday.'

She has just turned 75.

'We'll have to go to the mud pool place,' she says. 'Then you choose one thing and I'll choose one.'

He leaves her to it. In the corridor he is passed by several small children, wet and wrapped in pink towels, running ahead of a parent. A blackboard in the lobby bears the chalk inscription, *Kids! Superman 2 in video lounge 4.30.* At the desk a man who looks like an airline steward is issuing towels.

He turns left through french windows and finds himself in a spacious courtyard. Bamboo clumps, shrubs and patio tables. Children wriggle at the shallow end of a curved swimming pool. At the deep end men and women float against the edge, their arms along the railing like boxers resting between rounds.

A Chinese woman in a straw hat sits disconsolately in a smaller, square pool. A notice indicates that it is a spa pool but that the agitator is out of order. A third pool, even smaller — it might hold two people at a pinch — gives off a sulphurous stench. Robert touches his fingers into the water and quickly lifts them away. The heat is surprising. He reads a long notice which has two paragraphs about the health-giving qualities of the water and two about the precautions which the hotel would like to recommend because of possible dangers to health.

Next morning they park the car in Tryon Street. His mother makes her way through the drizzle towards a little cluster of souvenir shops. In the window of the shop she enters, a fat kiwi lazes in a deckchair, staring through sunglasses at a blue ocean horizon. A New Zealand flag waves above him. At his feet a handwritten sign says, *Customers wanted, please apply in shop.*

His mother is picking up and putting down items made from paua shell. Key-rings, ashtrays, coasters, lucky horseshoes, nail clippers, a game of noughts and crosses.

'Aren't they *clever*,' she says. The shop is an adventure.

On the wall behind her is a large poster, a map which shows New Zealand grown astonishingly large, mainly because Australia has been drawn as a tiny island off to the left. Perhaps he should get it for Peter – it might look amusing in a Sydney flat.

'Of course, you can just pick them up at the beach,' his mother says.

It might not be the right sort of thing. People prefer to make their own jokes. He didn't think he knew his son especially well. He didn't know what amused him really. But he ought to find something. He had felt absurd embarrassment at the airport when he realised he had no farewell gift, and then had felt silly for feeling he ought to have one. Only after Peter had gone through immigration did he notice the airport gift shop, its mugs with kiwis, its shirts with sheep. But he had driven back to Browns Bay.

On a shelf in front of him are rulers and chessboards made of native woods. There is a pencil case, like the one he was given when he started primary school, which he decides to buy. He will also buy some sachets of 'Miracle Mud — from the natural boiling pools in New Zealand's "Thermal Wonderland" '.

'Thank you, sir,' says the assistant.

'That's a good one,' his mother says. She is looking at a sign which says, *We have trained our souvenirs not to touch children; please train your children not to touch the souvenirs.* She does not buy anything.

A pale blue plastic comb is floating in a hot pool called Te Weranga — 'the place where someone was burned'. The drizzle comes and goes. They keep their umbrellas up.

His mother has a pair of poi looped around her neck. They look like bulbs of garlic, except that they are orange. She bought them 10 minutes ago from a 10-year-old girl. She has taken a photograph of the girl, standing next to Robert, in front of her stall. A condition of sale.

They come to the model pa but go quickly across to the carving centre where they can be out of the rain. This is also the main entrance to Whakarewarewa. Coaches are parked in the distance.

They join a line of people moving slowly along a walkway which skirts the outside of the carving workshop, a room marginally larger than their hotel bedroom. Three men tap with chisels, working on pieces which are at different stages of completion. One piece is barely begun — a length of wood with lines marked on the surface. The trainee carvers are all young, about Peter's age. From time to time they break off and stare at the piece on which they are working. It is hard to tell if they are inventing or remembering.

Out in the vestibule a young man in blue shorts and red jandals points with proprietorial pride at a carved wall panel. He must have made it. But the friend with him has the same gaze of satisfied ownership.

Where is his mother? Robert scans the tour groups who are gathered around women working with flax and feathers. 'And so we are spreading knowledge of these ancient arts,' a guide says. His mother has gone through into the souvenir area.

She has bought six copies of a postcard showing five small Maori boys, each naked, each poking out his tongue, each making a haka gesture with one hand while the other hand modestly covers (or clutches?) his genitals. She takes them out of the packet to show him.

Below the model pa the route loops past a Kiwi Nocturnal House. *Night conditions exist. Keep silent. No smoking. No photos.*

He follows his mother through two sets of doors and enters a dark curve crammed with bodies. There is loud, excited talking and a smell of dampness. Children are tapping on the glass window.

'Here it is,' cries a man. 'Over here!'

Robert looks but can see nothing. Dark branches.

'Here it is,' cries a voice like his mother's. 'Over here!'

He looks but can see neither the kiwi nor his mother.

Ten minutes later they are walking past the geysers. Are they playing? Steam drifts indistinctly through the rain. They walk back down through the white raised tombs of the small Catholic cemetery, cross a bridge and pass out through the archway which commemorates the dead.

It is the proud claim of the Tuhourangi people that on the outbreak of the Second World War all the men in the village between the ages of 16 and 60 years enlisted for overseas service. The memorial arch at the entrance to Whaka tells the story of their contribution to the wargod, Tumatauenga.

'Twenty-five *naughty* boys,' his mother says in the car, admiring her postcards. 'Did you see these, Robert?'

Then she says, 'I never liked the way your father put his tongue in my ear.'

Robert does not remember his father, who was in the engine room of the *Achilles* and died at sea two days out from Auckland. It had been a heart attack. 21 February 1940. The *Achilles* was sailing home to a heroes' welcome after the Battle of the River Plate. Robert's mother had travelled all the way to Auckland to be among the 100 000 people gathered to cheer the ship's company as they marched up Queen Street. She had waited in the crowd, unaware of her husband's death. Much later, she seemed to remember the thrill of the parade more vividly than her subsequent distress. She was interested in the grief but no longer felt it. Robert had been two. He had been left with some people in Dunedin.

'One thing at least is certain,' wrote Captain Parry, commander of the *Achilles*. 'The continued enthusiasm and cheerfulness, both in dull moments and in more exciting ones, of a predominantly New Zealand ship's company has been a revelation, and for four anxious days an inspiration to one who was bred and born in the Old Country. Though many weary and anxious times lie ahead, he feels complete confidence that such men cannot fail to win the final victory.'

Robert has no memory of his father — except for an impression, refined over many years, of what must once have been a dream. He is in a rowing boat with a smiling man in naval uniform. They are on a lake, the day is nearly over. The man explains that they are going to the island to see how the other children are getting on. 'Nearly there,' he sometimes says, 'nearly there.' Darkness and moonlight drip from his oars.

They drive quickly around the Government Gardens but do not leave the car. Robert's mother has run out of film. He parks the car on one of the shopping streets and dashes through rain towards a doorway.

He is in a colourful shop. A big man behind the counter is wearing an Argentine rugby jersey. It is too small for him. He is beef and teeth, a puma snarls beneath his collar. 'Ours is a speciality emphasis,' he says. He is sorry. Rosettes, yes, ties, replica jerseys, novelty cutlery — but no films. Behind him a sign says, *Shoplifters get court.* 'Up the road,' he says, and gestures up the road.

Robert tells his mother they will get a film at Rainbow & Fairy Springs. This is the tourist attraction he has picked out. First, though, they lunch at Springs Cottage. A filled roll for Robert, and a cream bun which seems to taste of chicken; a Devonshire tea for his mother. The rain comes and goes. Cars drive away, others pull up.

Entering Rainbow Springs they pass through another souvenir area. They get a film, then go on and gaze at pools of fish. They walk along bush trails, gazing from bridges and platforms, looking through underwater viewing windows. Rainbow-striped umbrellas jostle above the heads of the visitors. Children tug and quarrel beneath them, clutching bags of fish-food. There is another kiwi house, which Robert decides not to enter. He tells his mother he will wait for her in the souvenir shop. Rain on the gravel walkways.

He decides to buy another pencil case.

'I saw it,' says his mother. 'What do you want another one of those for?'

'I thought I might send it to Peter.'

'The time for that,' says his mother, 'was when she took him off.'

'She' is his ex-wife, Lorraine. Robert is Lorraine's ex-husband. Peter, he supposes, is his ex-son.

'It's just sentimental,' he says. 'Something I remember. A bit like your clothes-pegs.'

Robert is changing the subject. On her mantelpiece his mother keeps seven clothes-pegs. She won them when 'It's in the Bag' came to Lumsden. She should have taken the money.

Robert can still remember the entry for Lumsden in *Wise's New Zealand Index* ('every place in New Zealand, 9th edition'). He once learned it by heart. He wrote it out in a letter to his Australian penfriend.

> A town district and railway junction, on Oreti River; 50 miles north from Invercargill. Southland County. Sheep and dairy farming. Excellent trout fishing in Oreti River and good shooting. Splendid roads for motoring. Three good hotels. Post, telegraph, and money order office. Population, 510. The old name of this place was The Elbow.

Robert's mother worked as a housemaid-waitress at the Railway Hotel. 'Not live-in,' she occasionally said. She and Robert had their evening meal there, even on nights she wasn't working. It was always a roast, they always walked home together afterwards.

Robert's mother buys a teatowel with a spray of pohutukawa on it. She would like to go back to the Randwick now for a rest. Last night they ate at Pizza Hut. Tonight they are going to eat at McDonald's.

They are early at the Agrodome, a good half-hour before the morning show begins. They wander about in the sheepskin shop, occasionally peering out at the grey weather. Robert's mother picks up handknitted jerseys, exclaiming at the prices.

Robert browses in a booklet, *New Zealand and Its Sheep*, by Godfrey Bowen. Godfrey Bowen is a champion shearer who helped found the Agrodome. He writes lyrically of the farmers and shepherds of the world. They know no strikes, their work is like a calling. He speaks, too, of 'Mum', the farmer's wife. She feeds the family, fixes a broken garage door, drives the tractor,

7

takes telephone messages. She makes the farmhouse a haven of peace.

Robert's mother tugs him into the hall. She wants a seat at the front. The hall fills up behind them.

'Is there anybody here from Scotland?' calls the bush-singleted compère. 'What about Ireland? Spain? The Old Country?'

One by one he calls off the nations of the earth.

'Is there anybody here from the South Island?' Robert's mother makes a faint noise in her throat, half lifting a hand. Roars of self-acclaim come from the back rows.

'Is there anybody here from Japan?' Silence greets this query, although Robert can see a party of Japanese tourists on the other side of the aisle. In fact one has got to his feet now, but only to take a photograph.

'Welcome one and all,' says the compère, 'whatever part of this great planet you hail from.' He explains that his name is Colin, and that the parade of rams will now take place. A taped commentary by Godfrey Bowen will accompany the presentation. Then he will shear a sheep.

There are 19 rams, each representing a different breed. One by one they clatter into position on a set of tiered ramps, tempted by some sort of granulated feed in a canister whose lid is released by a pretty girl. As each ram begins snuffling in its canister, she chains it in place. Meanwhile Godfrey Bowen declares the breeds and countries of origin, adding something about the history and characteristics of each breed. The breeds of ram seem to be named after English towns and counties: Lincoln, Leicester, Suffolk, Dorset. The rams have their own names, too. Trotting one by one from opposite sides of the stage to be locked into position by the pretty girl come Rajah, Duke, Monarch, Sultan, Sambo. A bored merino ram called Prince has pride of place at the top of the pyramid.

Colin spreads his arms. People stand to take photographs. Others applaud.

Colin reaches into a pen and drags out a ewe. He wrestles it to its back. 'Wool,' he says. 'As old as time, as modern as tomorrow.'

As he shears, he calls out interesting facts. New Zealand leads the world in grasslands farming. Revolutionary techniques in top-dressing and pasture control mean that grass will grow for 11 months in most parts of the country. There are 30 sheep for each man, woman and child in New Zealand. There are 70 million sheep all told, of which 50 million are breeding ewes — 'like this lady here.'

There is an in-gasping moan from some members of the audience as a bright fleck of blood appears on the ewe's belly. Then there is a sprinkling of applause. Flashlights flash. The ewe is released into the rainy paddocks.

Colin raises the cloudy fleece above his head.

'Just like peeling a banana,' he says. 'I can tell you, ladies and gentlemen, the shearer works fast. Any decent sort of shearer would get through, oh, 300–350 sheep a day. And that's currently at about 61 cents a fleece around these parts.'

Because of the rain there will be no sheepdog demonstration, but a dog called Smoko bounds up the backs of the rams, leaping from one to another until he settles barking on the back of Prince the merino. Prince looks bored and sits down. The pretty girl tugs him to his feet. There will now be a period for formal photographs. The man Colin, the dog Smoko, and the ram Prince will be only too happy to pose with members of the audience. A queue quickly forms. Robert's mother insists that he join it. 'Smile,' she says.

Robert relaxes in the pool at the Randwick, thinking vaguely that he still has not seen the lake. His mother is lying down in their room, pleased with the Agrodome. 'The best of the lot,' she has decided. 'They all have their personalities, don't they?' She means the rams.

The pool is empty. The children and their parents have gone. A few pink abandoned towels. Tomorrow the police will come. Robert remembers something Peter told him over their drink in the airport bar. He was trying to bring to mind a moment he half recalled from childhood. Robert had taken him to the local swimming pool and had cradled him all the way from one side of

9

the deep end to the other. It was the first time he had been in at the deep end.

Robert cannot remember the occasion. Perhaps it had been a friend of Lorraine's, though he took care not to make the suggestion to Peter. It is impossible to know how much an experience means to another person. What will his mother remember about Rotorua?

(In 10 days' time Robert's mother will send him a colour photograph. On the back will be written, in her careful hand: *Robert and his 'royal friend'*. Prince's look of boredom will be exactly as Robert remembers. Robert's face will show an almost unimaginable happiness.)

Meantime there is the problem of where to eat. Perhaps they will try a hangi at one of the hotels. He floats on his back. He is pleased with himself: by accident he has stolen Godfrey Bowen's book about New Zealand sheep. It is in the car glovebox. 'The next book I write will be of my life, when I can go into more detail.'

A memory comes to him, unbidden, of his mother at the big wooden table in the kitchen at Lumsden. Sometimes she would earn extra income by colour-tinting the aerial photographs taken by one of the local top-dressing pilots. They were large black-and-white images, each with a farmhouse at the centre. Eventually they would hang in the farmhouses they represented.

The tiny brushes and little bottles of water-colours are spread out around her. Her name is Eileen Taylor. Her hand dips and hovers, she works with patience and precision. She does the roofs of houses and outbuildings first — red or green, sometimes orange. Then she colours the farm roads a putty yellow.

Picking out the highlights, it is called. Stands of pine and macrocarpa windbreaks are tinted green, creeks and ponds become an unreal blue. The paddocks are left grey, stretching out to the edges of the frame.

PONIES

IT WAS JUST AFTER the assassination of Indira Gandhi that I came into the employ of Jason Michael Stretch. Wellington is a city of hidden steps and narrow passages, dark tributary corridors which are rapidly being translated, courtesy of the new earthquake codings, into glittering malls and arcades, whole worlds of space-age glass and silver. Inside these places, on their several levels, there is a curious calm, which is now beginning to extend out on to the footpaths. No one points excitedly; people drift along, pale, ice-cold, gazing into windows in a way which is almost tranquil, or ride escalators which take them up and down but not quite anywhere. A few years ago — as, say, a first-year student — I think I might well have scorned these aimless citizens, or felt sorry for them: a bit superior, anyway. Now they strike me as somehow beyond distress or temptation or anyone's genuine concern — as if they are busy at something which the city itself expects of them, and which they do rather well merely by moving from one place to the next.

A few people behave as if they know their way around. They lack the general air of glazed serenity. They don't quite merge into the crowd. They move marginally faster, like swimmers going downstream, outpacing the current; then they duck clear and vanish into a doorway or make a sudden dash across the road into the downtown traffic. For a few weeks I was running so many errands for Jason Stretch that I began to fancy that I myself must have looked like this. A man who stood out a little from the crowd. A *busy* fellow, someone with intentions and a destination.

Pepperell and Stretch was in Upper Cuba Street — down an alleyway, up a flight of steps, several turns along a corridor. The footpath in that part of Cuba Street has a richness which not only assaults your nostrils, it manages to hit you right at the back of the throat — as if having soaked up a full variety of human juices over

11

the years it is eager to give something back. (You will see that in my weaker moments I would like to be a writer, not a part-time student of anthropology who has got himself lost somewhere between courses.) But maybe it is only because of the Chinese restaurant on the corner that someone with a spraycan has written Pong Alley just next to Drop the Big One — two messages which I had the opportunity to contemplate several times a day as I went by lugging a bag filled with items for the mail or yellow leaflets for one of Jason's suburban letterbox runs.

There wasn't a Pepperell, not in the office. One of my jobs, though, was to take the Number 1 bus out to Island Bay once a week and remove from the letterbox of a house in Evans Street the about-to-be-current issue of *Pepperell's Investment Weekly*, a stockmarket tip sheet, all immaculately typed and centred on a sheet of white A4 paper. Then the thing would be to take this back to town, over to Easiprint in Taranaki Street, and get 57 copies run off ('Pepperell and Stretch's charge account thanks'); and that same day if there was time, or the next morning if there wasn't, I'd trundle back out to Evans Street, ring the doorbell, go and stare at the island for half an hour — and back again to find each of the 57 sheets signed, 'All the best! Bob Pepperell', in a ragged blue ballpoint.

Mrs Watson said that the woman before her had told her that Jason had acquired *Pepperell's Investment Weekly* when he took over the firm, and that he had actually been a subscriber himself when he was still in Balclutha. Mrs Watson typed subscriber addresses on envelopes for me to slide the individually signed sheets into. She did one or two other jobs of the same sort; otherwise she typed student theses, paying Jason Stretch a 20 percent commission fee. She said this figure was 'very fair'. Jason looked after the horoscopes himself.

'A terrible business, this shooting in India,' said Jason Stretch. 'Two of Mrs Gandhi's bodyguards shot her seven times as she was walking from her home to an interview with the British actor Peter Ustinov. One of the assassins had been one of Mrs Gandhi's bodyguards for eight years. The entire security unit of Mrs

Gandhi's residence has been taken off duty and is undergoing intensive questioning. Unquote.'

He put down the *Dominion* and reached across the desk. I reached out my hand, since this was what he seemed to be expecting, and he took it. He shook it. (Was the grasp firm or limp?) 'Executed in cold blood by her own employees,' he said. 'These all have to be read for clipping and filing.' He gestured towards a pile of newspapers. 'Still, I doubt if you'll have time for that sort of thing. I very much hope you won't. Well, there we are. Nine o'clock tomorrow, then. Let's see how things go, Kevin.'

Well, there we were. As they say. I am inventing the words, for I have no clear memory of what they actually were. But I am doing my best to reconstruct the *tone* that I recall. Jason Stretch's communications to his employees (me and Mrs Watson) tended to jump about a lot but were somehow without energy or final form.

I had been expecting some sort of interview but apparently the job was mine. 'Editorial and administrative responsibilities,' the ticket at the job agency had said: 'Applicants must be steady and reliable but should also be comfortable with innovative thinking.' Apart from rotten pay, this added up to the expeditions out to Island Bay; a lot of time spent sitting in an old armchair next to Mrs Watson's desk and doodling on a clipboard; and looking after the post — which meant at least one cable-car ride a day up to the Kelburn Post Office to clear the private box which Pepperell and Stretch kept there.

Then there were the leaflet runs in the afternoons. 'But nothing too arduous,' said Jason Stretch. 'The experience of walking the footpaths is going to stand you in good stead I'm sure, but there's no point in wearing yourself out.'

Here he comes, the suburban packhorse . . .

Some afternoons I took a sheet advertising *Pepperell's Weekly*, and sometimes I had one headed 'Astral Readings!', which started off with a whole lot of stuff about the Future and ended with an invitation to write in confidence at once, giving your date of birth.

'Send no money now but be sure to include a stamped addressed envelope for immediate return of your free Astral Interpretation. Confidentiality guaranteed. Jason M. Stretch.'

The 'Jason M. Stretch' bit was a genuine signature. Each leaflet was individually signed. Jason spent a couple of hours every morning writing his name at the foot of his promotional leaflets. Perhaps it made him feel he existed more securely, perhaps the personal touch was company policy. Perhaps it came down to the same thing.

An odd thing: I must have glimpsed Jason's signature any number of times in an afternoon, but unless I was actually looking directly at it I could never summon up an image of it. Was it large or small? Neat? Listless? A jovial flourish? What colour ink?

Come to that, as I trailed around suburban Wellington, pushing Astral Readings into the letterboxes of Kilbirnie or Thorndon or Hataitai, I couldn't quite summon up Jason himself, I couldn't get him plainly in the forefront of my mind. He was in his late thirties, I'm pretty sure, certainly a good deal older than me. His hair was shortish, fairish . . . but was he balding or just closely cropped? Did he wear glasses all the time, or only for reading? Now I find myself wondering if he wore glasses at all.

All I can call into being is the outline of a body and a head above a desk. There is no colour which I associate with the eyes of Jason Stretch, or with his complexion; not even with his clothing. He barely has being, for all the hundreds of times he wrote his name.

He ought to have seemed to me then — and no doubt ought to seem to me now — grotesque, colourfully Dickensian; but he is ordinary and indeterminate and unemphatic, like a dark brown desk viewed against a light brown wall, like the office furniture he sat at.

So there we were, and the truly grotesque discovery was learning that Jason's occasional references to the value of walking had a point. During January and February, he thought, I might like to lead small walking tours around Wellington. All the major cities had them, he said. There were more people than you might imagine — tourists, visitors from out of town — who *liked* to move around a city more or less at ground level, maintaining a leisurely, unhurried pace, yet all the while being kept amused and informed by knowledgeable and entertaining guides.

Jason already had two tours mapped out ($15 a head) and some provisional copy for the brochures. 'Historic Thorndon: a leisurely ramble through pioneer Wellington — home of prime ministers, birthplace of Katherine Mansfield.' 'Harbour City: come with us on a stroll around Wellington's busy waterfront; see views of the harbour that even Wellingtonians don't see; visit the historic Maritime Museum.'

'We'll improve the descriptive stuff; it needs to sound about two hours' worth, wouldn't you say? How's "Secret Wellington" coming along, Kevin?' 'Secret Wellington' was a walk which Jason felt we needed to have up our sleeve in case Wellington's weather made 'Historic Thorndon' and 'Harbour City' doubtful prospects. An indoor, under-cover route which stuck to Lambton Quay, Willis Street and Manners Street (for example) would be just the thing.

'Keep it in mind as you go about the city, Kevin. All the little nooks and crannies. A few historic sites. Some of the new malls and plazas. What about the new BNZ underground place? There might be something there. Check it out when you go for the post.'

So there we were, me and my prospects, sitting on the cable-car in mid-November, worrying about January and how I could possibly handle the problem of knowing enough to be able to say anything at all to tourists and out-of-towners. And what if I bumped into someone I *knew* on one of these outings? I whimpered inwardly.

'You can always take them on the cable-car,' a small inner voice whispered to me; and I suddenly knew what it meant to be able to say that your whole being glowed with pleasure. I turned over one of the airmail letters which came addressed to Jason Stretch from Pundit Tabore, 'India's Most Famous Astrologer', of Upper Forjett Street, Bombay, India. I beamed at it in all its beauty. The flimsy brown envelope blazed out with coloured stamps. There was a woman doing gymnastic movements against a sky-blue background; against a red background a powerfully muscled man lifted weights. Five linked rings: the Olympics! But the odd thing about Pundit Tabore's letters (and here it was again) was that the stamps were always on the wrong side of the envelope. I mean, on one side of the envelope the man grunted and strained and the woman was graceful, while on the other was Jason M. Stretch's name and Wellington address.

'They always seem to get through, though,' said Mrs Watson. She was taking a break between chapters of a Communication Studies thesis. 'It must be their way of doing it. I'd love to know what that Indian's telling him.'

'Do you think he believes in it?' I said.

'Well,' said Mrs Watson, 'there must be about a dozen inquiries each week, and three or four of them end up sending the $75 for the full reading. I suppose they must learn something to their advantage. You need the place of birth for that, though, and the time of day as near as you can get it.'

Next morning I mentioned the cable-car to Jason.

'Well Kevin,' he said, 'let's hang fire on that one just for a little while, shall we?'

He seemed tired, but very excited.

'You know,' he said, 'an old bloke in the Catlins once told me that if you're a real bushman and it's about to rain, then you can hear the drops hitting the leaves at least a couple of minutes before the rain itself starts coming down. Even before it starts spitting, that is. Well,' he said, his voice pleased and lowered and confidential, 'I like to think I can hear people who are about to spend their money in just the same way. You can quote me on that when I'm famous.'

Of course, I am inventing the detail of Jason Stretch's words again, but not, you may be sure, out of nothing. Jason needed words like these as background and preamble to his main point, which was that he had seen on television the night before a panel discussion about nuclear winters. He had seen a way of making money.

'Horrifying. Makes you think. But it's a chance at last to combine real service to society with our own information skills.

And it means real research work for you, Kevin. You'll have to move quickly, though.'

There must have been a look of reluctance on my face.

'I grew up in Balclutha,' he said, 'but here I am' — as if this would solve whatever it was that was making me so diffident.

He was jumping up and down like the man who invented hokey-pokey ice cream.

I sat in the Wellington Public Library, researching survival techniques in sub-zero temperatures. I read about the Antarctic. Mrs Watson's uncle had watched the *Terra Nova* sail from Lyttelton in 1910.

'He said it was the next best thing to Noah's Ark. I never was much interested in the dogs really, it's the ponies I feel sorry for.'

'Ponies? I said.

NUCLEAR WINTER
War between the superpowers grows more and more likely every day!

It is well known that in the event of a nuclear exchange human life will become extinct in many areas of the planet.

Are you aware that things may be nearly as bad outside the immediate blast areas? Do you know that even a small nuclear war in the Northern Hemisphere may spell disaster in the South?

Smoke from fires burning in hundreds of cities will spread rapidly into the troposphere and stratosphere, severely limiting the amount of heat reaching the earth's surface from the sun.

A thick sooty pall. Darkness at noon. Temperatures will plummet. Imagine the cold and ice of an Antarctic winter. Many plant and animal species will be threatened with extinction. Many communities in the Northern Hemisphere will perish from the extreme cold.

In the Southern Hemisphere some of us may survive. Within three days, scientists have forecast, concentrated jet streamers of smoke and pollutants will have poured into the atmosphere above Australia and New Zealand. Those sufficiently prepared to cope with the sudden fall in temperature may win through, but many will not — the problem is beyond the limited resources of Civil Defence. The only answer is individual initiative and forward planning.

Write at once for your 'Nuclear Winter Kit'. It contains information essential to your personal survival. Make sure you will be ready to meet all eventualities. You owe it to yourself. You owe it to your children. Send $29.95 (cheque or postal order) to 'Nuclear Winter Foundation', Box 831-240, Wellington 5. We will send your 'Nuclear Winter Kit' by return post.

There were 19 Manchurian ponies on board the *Terra Nova,* taken to Antarctica to haul sledges. They were crammed aboard the tiny ship. 'One takes a look through the hole in the bulkhead,' wrote Scott, 'and sees a row of heads with sad, patient eyes come swinging up together from the starboard side, whilst those on the port swing back; then up come the port heads, whilst the starboard recede.' The ponies' boxes were two or three feet deep in manure when the *Terra Nova* came in sight of Antarctica.

The ponies were Manchurian, white or (a few of them) dappled grey. They cost £5 each. Captain Oates, famous for other things, was hired to look after the ponies. There are photographs taken by Ponting of the ponies aboard ship and on the ice. They are so white, the ponies, that they must often have been hard to see against the landscape they had been taken to.

There is a photograph of Oates standing on the upper deck of the *Terra Nova* with four of the ponies. Man and animals are all perfectly still, posed for the image. Among the shore photographs there is one of a pony called Chinaman with his leader, Wright. Wright faces the camera while Chinaman is in profile. There is a photograph of Oates standing with Snippets. There is Cherry-Garrard with his pony, Michael, of whom he said, 'Life was a constant source of wonder to him.' Michael is rolling on his back in the snow. Cherry-Garrard holds him on a long rein.

The ponies are greyish-white against the massive surround of ice and sky. They have coal-black eyes. The men are darker. The ponies seem to be moth-eaten; but maybe this is an effect of Ponting's photographs, or of the very rough photocopies which I made of them.

'A bit of fine tuning, but it's mostly there,' said Jason. 'We won't worry about any suburban deliveries with this one. People will be flocking into town for Christmas shopping over the next few weeks. We'll distribute directly, pass the stuff out in central Wellington.'

(Bowers records somewhere that old pony droppings, distorted by a trick of the Antarctic light, could look like a herd of cattle on the horizon.)

Oates was the man who looked after the horses. He was a taciturn man, known as Soldier, who wrote letters to his mother. He gave two lectures on the management of horses to the men wintering over in Antarctica, ending each with a joke or anecdote. On the journey to the glacier he wrote: 'Scott realises now what awful cripples our ponies are, and carries a face like a tired sea boot in consequence.'

Of the original 19 horses, only 10 were alive when Scott and his party set out on their journey to the Pole. Some had died on board the *Terra Nova* on its journey to Antarctica. Some had died on overland training trips. Others fell from ice floes into the ocean.

Only 10 survived the winter and all of these were to be shot when the sledge parties reached the Beardsmore glacier; subsequently the men would haul their own sledges. The ponies were old, at the end of their working life; they had been bought cheap by a man who knew nothing about horses. 'Poor ancient little beggar,' Bowers wrote of Chinaman, 'He ought to be a pensioner instead of finishing his days on a job of this sort.'

On 24 November 1911, Jehu was shot. His body was cut up and given to the dogs.

On 28 November, Chinaman was shot. Oates remarks, 'He was

a game little devil, and must have been a goodish kind of pony fifteen years ago.'

Scott and his men were now having pony meat in their hoosh. They found it much improved.

On 1 December it was the turn of Christopher, a pony who had been 'nothing but trouble', requiring four men to hold him down whenever his harness was to be placed upon him. 'He was the only pony who did not die instantaneously,' wrote Cherry-Garrard. 'Perhaps Oates was not so calm as usual, for Chris was his own horse though such a brute. Just as Oates fired he moved, and charged into the camp with a bullet in his head. He was caught with difficulty, nearly giving Keohane a bad bite, led back and finished.'

Oates now took over the leading of Scott's pony, Snippets. Scott roved about on skis, photographing the ponies as he went.

The next pony shot was Victor. Bowers wrote: 'Good old Victor! He has always had a biscuit out of my ration, and he ate his last before the bullet sent him to his rest.'

On 4 December Michael was dispatched.

A disastrous blizzard raged for several days. On 9 December the party reached the glacier. It had been a 14-hour march. One member of the party later recalled the condition of the ponies, 'Their flanks heaving, their black eyes dull, shrivelled, and wasted. The poor beasts stood,' he wrote, 'with their legs stuck out in strange attitudes, mere wrecks of the beautiful little animals that we took away from New Zealand.'

The last five ponies were shot on 9 December.

When Scott and his party were dispatching the remaining ponies, more than a month of overland sledge-hauling lay ahead of them. Amundsen would reach the Pole in a matter of days. It was Oates's work with the ponies which so impressed Scott that he asked him to join the smaller team which now made the ill-fated final 'dash'.

Rajiv Gandhi stood by his mother's flaming funeral pyre, surrounded by the dignitaries of the world.

20

As the flames spread, India's new Prime Minister stood with his hands clasped in prayer, receiving the condolences of official mourners. Behind barriers, tens of thousands of people also mourned the death of the woman they knew as Mother India.

Nearly an hour after setting the pyre ablaze, Rajiv was still on the surrounding platform waiting according to Hindu custom for the body's head to explode.

Mourners touched their foreheads to the platform.

'Tomorrow,' said Jason Stretch, 'I think we'd better make a start on distributing these, Kevin.'

There were half a dozen big cartons of leaflets.

'I very much hope we'll need to run off a few more than this before we're finished. I think the thing will be to stick around the new shopping plazas. And we'll need to begin finalising copy for the Kit itself. How's it coming along?'

I said that I'd picked up quite a lot of material on some of the Antarctic expeditions.

'Right. And it might be worth checking with Civil Defence. They may have a few words of advice. Or tramping clubs and things like that. There must be plenty of stuff available. But see if you can get rid of a box of these first.'

I stood with my armful of leaflets outside the new AA building in Lambton Quay for 47 minutes before it came to me that I was never going to work up the courage to stick Nuclear Winter sheets under the noses of passing Christmas shoppers. At the same time I realised that it wasn't that I particularly disapproved of what Jason Stretch was up to. I probably did, but the real truth was that I felt silly — or was scared I would look silly. Each moment that went by, I felt a little more potentially ludicrous. From time to time someone would look at me curiously. I tried to look as though I was waiting for somebody. Help! I tried to stand there as though I wasn't there.

I wrote out my resignation on the back of a Nuclear Winter sheet and posted it to Jason's box number. 'All the best to Bob

Pepperell', I added. I dumped the pile of leaflets at the end of an empty counter in the Chews Lane post office. I don't know why I should have forgotten the ponies. You grow up knowing all that stuff about Scott and Captain Oates. Oates was in charge of the ponies. That's why he was there in the first place. They called him the Soldier. I am just going outside and I may be some time.

The ponies' names were James Pigg, Bones, Michael, Snatcher, Jehu, Chinaman, Christopher, Victor, Snippets and Nobby. After I had written Jason Stretch's name and address on the envelope, I stuck the stamp on the opposite side.

I actually saw Jason about half an hour after I'd posted the letter. He was on an escalator at the new BNZ Centre. I half tried to catch his eye, but he looked straight through me — not because he was choosing to ignore me but because he wasn't quite looking at anything. I can't remember now, just a few weeks later, whether he was rising up out of the earth or descending into it.

SIENA

THEY WERE TRAVELLING in a part of the country famous for its waterfalls. The waterfalls were named after Italian cities, apparently something to do with the new government. They had seen Firenze, a 10-minute walk through bush from a roadside parking lot. A double fan of feathery water: pretty, but nothing special.

It was Jazelle's idea to stop somewhere for a few days. Vicks was sick of the driving, so it suited her. And Lucas: who knew what Lucas thought? 'Wherever the road leads on,' he said. He had watched too many old movies. Another tablet fizzed on his tongue.

They had picked him up further down the coast. He had praised the colour of the car and offered himself as a travelling companion. It turned out that he wasn't good company, not in any respect at all really, but neither of the girls had had the heart to tell him. Vicks had come close a couple of times.

Late in the afternoon they found a small hotel. Two storeys, weatherboard, corrugated iron roof. In one direction there was the low whirr of the traffic-way, somewhere out of sight; in the other, a couple of paddocks. Beyond the paddocks the bush started. Off in the distance they could see a glacier, a glint of white.

The hotel toilets said 'Officers' Mess' and 'Powder Room'. On the back of a cubicle door Lucas stared at a rhyme:

> Here I sit all broken-hearted,
> Paid a penny and only farted.

He repeated it several times at dinner. 'Cheap at the price,' he said, giggling. 'A penny for your thoughts,' he said to the gloomy woman, presumably the publican's wife, who served them. The dining room had three tables, all set with cutlery, but there were no other guests. The woman brought them shepherd's pie and, to follow, instant pudding with sliced peaches. The hotel had a fifties emphasis.

The woman had given Vicks and Jazelle a twin room. Blue candlewick bedspreads. They pushed the two beds together. Lucas was by himself in a single along the corridor. You would think that was clear enough.

In one corner of the girls' room a Toogood stood blinking. Its display showed the word 'Burlap'.

'But what was the question?' said Jazelle. To no one in particular.

Lucas put his head around the door. He sidled in and squatted on his haunches. He switched the Toogood to audio.

'Who or what was Phar Lap?' said the Toogood.

Then it said, 'What is a Stevenson screen?'

Then, 'What is the name of the natural home of a beaver?'

'Just as well you don't have a throat,' said Lucas. He flicked open his knife and whispered to himself. His homicidal maniac display. His crazy stuff.

Quack. Vicks farting. *Quack. Quack.* When Vicks farted she made small quacking noises like a duck.

'Straight for the carotid,' said Lucas. 'Every time.' He put a Keepsake on his tongue and grinned as it melted.

Jazelle and Vicks descended to the bar.

Lucas waved his knife at the Toogood.

'What about, "a Canadian dam"?' he said. 'I'll say, "a Canadian dam".'

'Incorrect,' said the Toogood. For some reason it switched itself to hold.

'I'm 47,' said Lucas, 'too old for this sort of shit.'

The barman was the publican. 'R. P. Heron —Licensed to Sell Spirituous Liquors.' He wore a white shirt and braces. His face looked mildly disappointed above a tartan bow-tie.

'What's your pleasure?' said R. P. Heron.

The room was period decor. Grey lino underfoot, while the bar itself was surfaced in a kind of red formica. The beer came through hoses.

They stayed with the period. Jazelle ordered a Bacardi and Coke.

'Likewise,' said Vicks.

'If you insist,' said Lucas. 'Surprise surprise.'

'Quiet tonight,' said Jazelle.

R. P. Heron explained that the bar was closed except for bona fide guests. And it was mid-week in a slow time of year.

Vicks switched on the holovision. A Nana Mouskouri clone assembled herself.

'Thank you for welcoming me to your home,' she said. 'My music is like a beautiful rainbow. It has no frontiers, no barriers.'

Lucas moved across to the bar. A refill. A double Scotch.

'In my country we try to find a better tomorrow, and tears are mixed with laughter, joy holds hands with sorrow. We sing, dance, and clap hands as all the passions and sorrows come out.'

'That's a decade out,' said Lucas. 'At the very least. If it's the fifties you have in mind.' He placed a Keepsake on the centre of his tongue.

'I won't be arguing over that one,' said R. P. Heron. He swayed forward on his toes and gave a delicate shrug, like a diver on a high board. 'You do the best you can.'

Nana Mouskouri sang 'The White Rose of Athens'. She swayed as she sang. She walked towards Lucas.

Lucas reached out as if to pull her glasses off, but his hand passed through her head. She made a graceful exit through the wall.

'Steady on son,' said R. P. Heron.

Lucas was the only customer in the bar.

'Our finest hour,' said R. P. Heron. 'Home little bastards home.'

Lucas drifted outside and circumnavigated the hotel. Gravel crunched under his feet. The sky like an instrument panel.

Vicks and Jazelle were in their room. There was a light. Jazelle would be oiling Vicks. Starting with the back of the neck. And then the shoulders.

Upstairs again, he found their door was locked. They had

wheeled the Toogood through to his room. It was showing the word 'Mansfield'.

In the morning Jazelle said, 'I do believe it's time Lucas had a taste of the old heave-ho.'

Vicks looked out the window. There was a small jungle gym. A pet lamb was tied to it, and two boys were patting the lamb.

'Whatever you think,' she said. *Quack*.

They went down to look at the lamb. The boys were listening to it. It turned out to be one of the recent implants.

'Legends of the land', said the taller boy. 'The Sadness of Uenuku. Tawhaki the Bold. The Death of Maui.'

The lamb said, 'After that, each fighting man raised his right hand, in which he was holding his weapon, and held it to his eyes, as though shading them.'

'Rest,' said the smaller boy. Somewhere inside the lamb the voice cut out.

'So what do people do around here?' said Vicks.

'Go to the waterfalls,' said the taller boy.

'Go to the glacier,' said the other. 'Or the waterfalls.'

They aimed vaguely toward the glacier. The road wound up into the hills, sometimes smooth, sometimes bumping through its own potholes. Occasionally they clattered across a one-way bridge. The colour of the water varied, depending on the stream. Milky grey was probably the glacier.

In the back of the car, Lucas chattered on. He had remembered his first visit to the doctor which, now he came to think of it, was his only visit to a doctor. This was still in the days of stethoscopes, if the word meant anything at all.

'So he had this stethoscope thing hanging around his neck, eh, this *listening* device, and he put the ear bits in his ears and the plug end on my chest and listened to my heart beating. "So what can you hear?" I said. He took the plug bit off my chest and pressed it on the top of my head and said, "I hear each one of your very interesting thoughts." Interesting thoughts! My mother thought it was hilarious. I was rigid, absolutely rigid.'

Quack, said Vicks. The road dipped and twisted.

'I was so frightened I didn't know what I was thinking anyway.'

They went slowly uphill. A coach ground past them, hooting. Foreign tourists aimed their lenses. Lucas gave the fingers.

They stopped in a clearing in a beech forest. Lucas stayed in the car.

Someone was selling sandwiches off a trestle table. A girl sold hula hoops. Jazelle looked at them and asked was there only the green colour.

The girl demonstrated.

'When you get to 70 revolutions a minute,' she said, 'you go danger.'

She rotated her body inside the hoop. The hoop went faster and faster, then suddenly spun from green to red.

'Danger,' said the girl. 'As fast as that. Seventy-five dollars.'

They took the walk to the waterfall. Jazelle wore her hoop like a necklace. They looked at the unnaturally thin stream of black water, which descended through several ledges. Its name was Little Napoli. Somewhere there would be a Big Napoli. The water flowed off underground.

They drove to Palermo. There was a giant parking lot. Rows of tents and stalls, amusement parlours, all kinds of vendors.

'Hunger hunger,' said Lucas. Hangi food. Hot dogs. Kebabs. Vegan. He ambled off towards a stall with a large Keepsake sign above it.

Vicks gunned the motor. Vroom vroom.

Jazelle watched through the back window. Lucas had half turned and was watching them go. He held his right hand to his eye, as though shading them. But the sun was behind clouds.

They drove back slowly. Why hurry? A scenic route looped around the glacier. The road nudged its way through bush, below a jagged ridge of ice.

They stopped at a place for lunch, 'The Diggings', paying for a window view.

'It's in retreat,' said the waiter. He dressed their salads with his back to the glacier. 'They call it negative regime. Come back in 20 000 years.'

Back at the hotel the lamb was asleep. Last rays of afternoon sun.

Vicks tried the hula hoop but couldn't get started. She froze, her knees slightly bent. One of those things.

Jazelle was born for it. She could swing the hoop around her legs, her hips, her waist, her neck. She moved it up and down her body. Then she got up speed. The green slipped to red. But she couldn't hold it steady. The red came and went.

Vicks filmed her. The lamb in the background. Jazelle going in and out of danger.

Vicks and Jazelle sat over their soft drinks. No one else in the bar.

Talking of this and that. Where to go tomorrow.

The holovision was a man in a kilt. He played a piano accordion. The strains of 'Loch Lomond'.

'Surprise surprise,' said Lucas.

He had a Keepsake sway.

Lucas said, 'A double Scotch. And then a double Scotch.'

Vicks and Jazelle concentrated on their lemonade.

'Dinkum?' said R. P. Heron.

The accordion player stopped. He seemed to be out of breath. Mist, a point or two of light, nothing.

'I hitch-hiked down the valley,' said Lucas. 'Old fifties custom. I got a ride with these Italians.'

He put a Keepsake on his tongue.

'Well, goodnight Mr Heron,' called Vicks.

'You sort of remind me of people I used to know,' said Lucas. 'Mistral. Patchouli. Cumulonimbus. Just say the word.'

Lucas addressed R. P. Heron. 'Tell me,' he said, 'What is the Chandler wobble?'

'Well, I know very little about music as such,' said R. P. Heron.

'This appliance seems a little faulty,' said Lucas. He pointed to his empty glass.

'Steady on,' said R. P. Heron. 'I think you might be getting just a bit shickered. Next thing we'll be having to carry you up to your bed. If you aren't careful.'

'Listen,' said Lucas. 'Listen to me please. I am a real and

historical person, thoroughly researched and well presented. What's the problem?'

Vicks and Jazelle watching from the door.

Lucas with his knife out.

R. P. Heron touched a concealed button with his foot. A bell started ringing.

Lucas slid his knife into R. P. Heron's throat. Easy. R. P. Heron slumped over the bar. There was an oily smell, and a sort of pink liquid oozing from his throat.

Lucas went outside. Sky like an instrument panel. Vicks and Jazelle at their window.

The lamb bleated. Lucas cradled it. He put the point of the knife against its throat.

The lamb said: 'But Papa, the Earth, still loves Rangi, the Sky. And the white mists rise from earth to sky to tell the universe his love, while he weeps for her in the falling dew, and sighs for her in the moaning wind.'

Years later, when they were all in different places, this is how things were.

Whenever Jazelle saw a duck, she remembered Vicks. Quack. And if Vicks saw a circle she might think of a hula hoop, and then she might recall Jazelle. Traffic lights could do it, too: the green and red.

And Lucas: Lucas thought of nothing. There was nothing on his mind.

Vicks and Jazelle never thought of Lucas. The Lucas memories had been over-recorded.

For example, if either of them saw a lamb, or even a picture of a lamb, there came at once to mind the image of a stream of water, falling. The name 'Siena' would float beneath it, like one of those subtitles you used to see in foreign movies. For a minute or two, while it lasted, Vicks and Jazelle would watch the display. Siena was beautiful — milky white and soundless — and it plunged in a single, long, unbroken column for what was apparently a record distance.

29

THERE IS A PHOTOGRAPH of early Dunedin, taken from the top of the Town Hall in 1883. It shows the lower side of the Octagon: the mouth of Lower Stuart Street to the left, of Princes Street to the right. In the middle distance, and probably the photographer's subject, First Church stands on its hillock. Beyond it you can make out reclaimed land and warehousing. Further off the masts of ships lift above the harbour.

The photograph was taken by John R. Morris. You can find it in a book of early Dunedin photographs from the Hardwicke Knight collection. 'People and vehicles,' says an accompanying note, 'have moved during the time exposure so that the streets appear empty.'

And it is true: the small town is like a child's model. Spires and shopfronts; a Sunday morning silence; a place which will never have a human population. It is possible to guess where people may have been: that faint blur, there, on the pavement; those marks that look like brush-strokes on the surface of the road. In fact, if you gaze carefully — as I am gazing now — you will see that one or two human figures have persisted. A tiny man stands outside Smith and Smith, next to a horse. On the corner of Princes Street and the Octagon another man stands in front of W. Absolon Smith, Tailor. He wears a dark suit and hat, and is staring intently towards the centre of the Octagon. He looks as if he is watching a procession, or waiting at a set of traffic lights. But of course in the Dunedin of 1883 there is no such thing as a set of traffic lights.

The lower half of the photograph is history. But the upper half is sky: a uniform white, a white wholly without blemish, intruded upon only by the slender, ascending spire of First Church. It is tempting to imagine that the photographer stared out from the top of the Dunedin Town Hall at a cloudless 19th-century blue:

cerulean. But there must have been clouds. They would have been moving too fast for the camera to take them in.

The Queen looks down from her high window above Princes Street. What a dump, she thinks. What a ghastly hole.

The empty streets.

Some man is telling her that Dunedin means 'Eden on the hill'. He is explaining that she is visiting a city of firsts.

The skirl of the pipes. A highland band goes by. *Snap*. The Queen takes a photograph. *Ho-ro you nutbrown maiden.*

Yes, says the civic dignitary, who stands slightly behind his monarch, speaking over her shoulder, we can for example lay claim to the nation's first university, the University of Otago, founded 1869.

A haka party goes by on the deck of a lorry. *Snap*.

We can also boast the first secondary school for girls, indeed the first in the Empire, 1870.

Commonwealth, says the Queen. She waves.

The empty streets. A brass band goes by. *Snap*.

The first woollen mills, 1874. The first daily newspaper, 1861. The first shipment of frozen meat home to the old country, aboard the ship named for our city, the *Dunedin*, 1882.

Marching girls. *Snap*. A band of assassins. *Snap*.

Why, says the civic dignitary, the list is endless.

I am told, remarks the Queen, that on its first voyage the *Dunedin* carried in all the carcasses of some 4 908 sheep and lambs.

I believe so, ma'am.

(The Queen is always extensively briefed on these visits.)

And that after nine further voyages the *Dunedin* was lost without trace in the year 1890, perhaps, some believe, having struck an iceberg off the Cape of Good Hope. And that she and all her complement and cargo now rest in a watery grave.

I believe so, ma'am. Also the first kindergarten, St. Andrew's Hall, 1889.

A line of lorries goes by. Local actors are dressed to represent the first professors of the University.

The Professor of Classics. *Snap*. The Professor of Mathematics,

31

at a blackboard. *Snap*. The Professor of Mental Science. *Snap*. The Professsor of English Language and Literature. *Snap*. The Professor of Natural Philosophy. *Snap*. Chemistry. *Snap*. Biology. *Snap*. Mining and Mineralogy. *Snap*. Anatomy and Physiology . . .

But the Queen has run out of film.

Ours too was the first School of Medicine in the land, says the civic dignitary. To us it fell also to appoint the first woman professor in New Zealand, Professor W. L. Boys-Smith, head of the faculty of Home Science.

But the Queen has run out of small talk.

She turns from the window and addresses one of her security men.

Tell me, she says, what has four legs and goes 'tick-tock'?

Ma'am?

A watchdog, says the Queen.

It could be anyone at all in that 1883 photograph, standing outside a tailor's shop on the corner of Princes Street and the Octagon, just across from the spot where the Star Fountain now plays music in the evenings. As it happens, I believe the man may be my great-grandfather, Priam Murphy, after whom I am named. A sense of remoteness makes him look older than the 33 years he would have been then.

In the photograph you can see that small trees and shrubs have been recently planted in the Octagon. I am almost certain it is these trees at which my great-grandfather is staring so intently. Each is encircled by a fence, about waist-high. Not much can be done about the wind, but at least the young trees can be protected from the depradations of browsing wagon-horses and wandering stock. Strange to say, the greatest danger comes from boys playing football. They do not care where they run, or on what they trample. There are no flowerbeds in the Octagon in 1883, and for good reason.

My great-grandfather is keeping an eye on the trees and shrubs. After all, he had a hand in planting them. It is a thankless task. Most passers-by find him amusing. Yet he will have his reward, although he does not know this yet.

Just at the moment, however, he cannot see the boys chasing after the flying ball. He cannot see the horse which suddenly panics when it is struck by a ball outside Smith and Smith. Everything is moving too fast to leave any impression.

In Great King Street, not far from the Captain Cook Hotel, there are several buildings which belong to the university's School of Medicine. The building with which I am associated has an official name and street number, but most people know it as 'The Sheep-Dip'. Few could tell you why. Most would say it was one of those funny, local names. Perhaps in early days settlers had a sheep-dip there . . .

The Sheep-Dip is seven storeys high. It has as many floors as Dunedin's — and New Zealand's — first skyscraper, the Mutual Funds Building, erected in 1910.

My name is Priam Murphy, and each day I make my way to the seventh floor of the Sheep-Dip to see to the current residents.

The room is large, rectangular. One wall boasts a portrait of the Queen, red-jacketed and side-saddle, on her horse Burmese. If, like John R. Morris 100 years ago, I want to look out across the city, I must clamber over the double aluminium farm gates which cut the room in two, edge my way past half a dozen drowsy sheep and stare out through a small window. Then there is a view of the far side of the harbour. Grey of water, green of hills, cloudy blue of sky. In front and to the right are hospital buildings. If I crane my neck a little, I can see to the left the Museum Reserve and the main entrance to the museum itself.

Each day I sweep and shovel shit away. Sheep have tidy droppings, so it is not a particularly messy business. I set down food — artificial mixtures, some of it in granule form, some of it a rough mash pudding which I make up myself from a base of pulped swede turnip. I examine scars and check for newcomers. I look to see who might be missing. How is Princess Anne today? And where is the Queen Mother?

I look under the straw, too, to see if anyone has tampered with the gun.

My name is Priam Murphy. I am a member of the university

ground staff. The sheep blink at me, their eyes full of dark reproach. As if I were the one who insisted on all this! As if I myself might raise the knife above them!

Yet they are right, I am culpable, I accept things as they are. My aunt does not. She says that I am her beautiful boy but I am one of those songs in which the melody gives advice to the words. I sing the song of circumstance, I do as the tune tells me.

Here is a true story which my aunt told me.

Not so long ago, a 17-year-old, Marcus Serjeant, was sent to prison for 5 years for firing a gun with intent to alarm the Queen. On Saturday 13 June 1981 the Queen was riding down the Mall for the annual ceremony of Trooping the Colour. Six pistol shots rang out. The Queen was courage itself; she kept control of her horse Burmese, which almost bolted.

Serjeant's gun contained blanks, and he was quickly subdued by angry members of the public. For a while his life was in considerable danger.

Serjeant had written to the Queen, warning her to stay at home on 13 June. 'There is an assassin out to get you.'

He described himself clearly. But no one saw him coming.

My great-grandfather, the first Priam Murphy, came to Dunedin from Melbourne in 1877. Like most others he was too late for the gold, but he knew a thing or two about seeds and plants, so hired himself out as a gardener and set up in business in a quiet way importing seeds and plants from England. By the mid-1880s he had his own retail outlet in George Street and a fairly large nursery in North East Valley. There are four bungalows on the old nursery site now. I live in one of them with my aunt. It is my house. I have taken her in. In some ways, I suppose, she has taken me in.

Remember Tangiwai, my aunt says.

It wasn't long before Priam Murphy had become an informal consultant to the city fathers, and one of the prime movers in the newly founded Amenities Society. It was the Amenities Society which successfully campaigned to have Dunedin's public reserves planted and properly tended. Many felt that the Octagon especially had become a mark of reproach, a blotch on a city whose whole originating impulse had been a vision of moral beauty. My great-grandfather worked in closely with the local councillors. It was he who decided on the Oriental plane trees for the Octagon, and the trees themselves — like those in Queens Gardens and the Museum Reserve — came through the North East Valley nursery. When the council brought David Tannock out from Kew Gardens as Superintendent of Parks and Reserves, Priam Murphy felt he had done his work. He watched from a distance as Tannock created the Botanical Gardens. He never voiced disapproval but there was something pointed about the speed with which he offered his services to the university, supervising two full-time groundsmen for only a small honorarium.

My great-grandfather was a man of ideas before he was a man of substance. It was he who dreamed up the first large shipment of hedgehogs in 1885. His scheme was mocked in the newspaper, but he was convinced the hedgehog would quickly adapt and come to control a wide range of garden pests. Time has proved him right. My aunt says that if she could have sixpence for every hedgehog in Dunedin, she would have enough money to move to Auckland.

My aunt is a frail, nondescript woman. In the street you would probably fail to notice her coming towards you. She has no more substance than a reflection in the window of Arthur Barnetts — a thin grey figure flitting through the new display of winter coats.

She loves jigsaws. She has just finished 'The Death of Captain Cook' and is making a start on a new one. At the moment she is sitting quite still, gazing at the image on the box. A tiny, two-masted ship is perched on the horizon near the middle of the painting. It is caught between a furious blue ocean and a sky of wild, unsteady grey. The ship seems the least important thing on view, though it attracts the eye.

The painter has called his picture 'The Days of Sail'. There are 1800 pieces.

The Queen visits Dunedin from time to time, although not as often as many citizens would like. In 1954 Leonard Wright got a knighthood out of it. But she made no sign of coming here on her latest New Zealand trip — something which many locals took as a personal slight, while others saw in it confirmation of the city's slow decline. The Queen preferred a swamp near Wellington. She stood on her wooden platform and saw, instead of swampbirds, the white helmets of crouching policemen.

But the Queen was in Dunedin on the afternoon of 14 October 1981, just a few months after the episode with Marcus Serjeant. Mid-October is a difficult time of year in Dunedin. Too late, certainly, for the rhododendrons at the Botanical Gardens, but a little early for the azaleas. Hence the decision to visit the Science Fair at the museum in Great King Street, just across the road from the Sheep-Dip.

My aunt is my mother's sister. Both girls were born in Auckland and came down here to study medicine. My mother fell in love with one of the university gardeners and for her that was the end of that. My aunt found she could not bear the separation from her sister, so came and lived with us, helping my mother keep house. I have a photograph of the family at St Clair. I am holding my aunt's hand. We are standing beside my mother who is buried up to her neck in the sand. We look pleased with ourselves, as if between us we have just invented the whole idea of a day at the beach. My father must have taken the photograph since he is nowhere to be seen.

My aunt does her jigsaws and likes the occasional sherry.

On becoming soldiers, she says, we do not cease to be citizens.

She sorts the pieces of her new jigsaw puzzle into two separate piles: one of cloud, one of water.

My aunt calls me her beautiful boy but I am nearly 50. I have a ginger beard, a barrel chest and am already quite bald. I do as the tune tells me, though I am far from musical. People tell me I look like a pirate. But I do not have a parrot on my shoulder.

I am an employee of the University of Otago, a minor member

of the ground staff. Both my father and my grandfather were Head Gardener, a position first created after the death of Priam Murphy. But I have not risen to such heights. I know nothing of plants and trees. I can tell a pine tree from a rose bush, but finer discriminations are beyond me. Through me the university maintains a family tradition; it also shows its sympathy in the matter of my father's death.

I do very ordinary jobs. I mow the lawns below the Clock Tower. I move compost to and fro in a wheelbarrow and throw weeds on the incinerator. Each day I go to the seventh floor of the Sheep-Dip. The half-dozen sheep, crossbred ewes and wethers, stare at me with dark, reproachful eyes. They think I am going to choose one of them for surgery. But it is tomorrow that Princess Anne will have her hysterectomy. It is tomorrow that Lord Snowdon will receive the kidney which was yesterday removed from Princess Michael.

It is not my job to get the country's medical students off to a good start in the world of surgery. That is not how I think of myself. No, I am here to pulp the swede turnip and remove the sheep droppings. I am here to worry about the gun, to wonder what it is for, and why no one else has seen it.

14 October 1981

The Queen and Prince Philip have flown to Dunedin. They drop out of the sky on a lightning visit. Within half an hour of their noon arrival they are in the midst of one of their habitual walkabouts, strolling informally in the Octagon, chatting to the Mayor about the agreeable spring weather, and admiring the plane trees which are just coming into leaf.

It is a time of special offerings. The Queen accepts posies and bouquets as they come to her, until her arms are full of flowers. One lady displays a tea-towel with a border of tiny Union Jacks. Another shows the Queen a large photograph of the Royal Family in July 1947, taken at the time of the Queen's engagement to Prince Philip. A small girl shows a picture of her kitten.

But there are discordant notes. Toward the end of the

walkabout there are representatives of the usual protest groups. Maori radicals. IRA sympathisers. Republicans. The unemployed. Lesbians. There are placards and banners. 'The Empire Is Dead'. 'Go Home Irihapeti'. Some of the demonstrators are chanting: 'Jobs not tours! Jobs not tours!' Loyal onlookers set up a rival cry: 'We love the Queen! We love the Queen!'

But the Queen does not hear. She has already been whisked off to lunch at the Southern Cross Hotel.

I have a cutting from the next morning's *Otago Daily Times*, which shows my aunt holding a photograph up before the Queen. The caption underneath reads *Yes, that's me!* The Queen is pointing and smiling, her arms are full of flowers.

I asked my aunt about this quite recently, and she said she felt she had to be absolutely sure.

Christmas Eve 1953. 10.21 p.m.

The Wellington-Auckland express plunges through a bridge into the suddenly swollen Whangaehu River, about a mile north of Tangiwai. There are 285 passengers aboard the train but only 134 survive.

My mother and father were planning to visit my mother's parents in Auckland. They had packed Christmas presents. They also hoped they might see the Queen there. They said they would tell her to look out for me when she got to Dunedin. They thought this was a great joke.

It is not clear why they set off to the North Island without taking me. I was 14. It was Christmas, a special time of year. Perhaps I didn't want to go. My aunt says that my mother said on the station platform that she needed a little fillip and my father said Elizabeth already had him.

It was confusing at the time and that is how it goes on. Everything runs together, caught up in the unimaginable mass of water which bore off bridge and carriages and stripped many victims of their clothes and shoes.

My parents left me a bicycle for Christmas. My mother's body was returned to Dunedin for burial. I never saw her. My father was never found. His was one of 20 bodies which were never accounted for. My aunt says he was probably swept out to sea. Even the train's carriages ended up several miles downstream. Shoes were being washed up on the beaches around Wanganui throughout 1954.

I ran up the stairs of the Sheep-Dip. I was probably too late, but all the same I ran.

The sheep were huddled in a corner, a chorus of worried bleats proceeding from expressionless faces. Beneath the window Princess Margaret lay unmoving on the straw. Her skull had been crushed, blood leaked from it.

I knelt beside her. All I could guess was a heavy blow.

A heavy blow all right. But where was the gun?

The Queen's car draws up outside the Otago Museum. The civic luncheon at the Southern Cross has gone off rather well. Now it is time to inspect the New Zealand Science Fair with its experimental exhibits showing research and technical skills in the fields of biological and physical sciences, and applied science and technology. Now it is time for the Queen to walk beneath trees planted by my great-grandfather 100 years ago.

Suddenly there is a loud report — like a firecracker, or a rifle shot. The Queen's police officer, Commander Trestrail, looks worried. Men around the royal car begin to reach into their inside jacket pockets.

But there is no need to panic. The Queen has heard nothing. It may only have been a metal traffic sign being knocked over. It may only have been a vehicle backfiring. The Queen steps from her car on to the footpath.

And the museum visit goes ahead without delay. The Queen is particularly tickled by a device entitled 'Mouse Power', showing mice running almost perpetually on a wheel to produce energy. On a more serious note, the Duke learns that the regional science fairs — there are now 13 of them — usually involve as many as 5 000 exhibitors, young and old, every year.

In all it is a brief but highly successful visit. Perhaps the only discordant note comes from the Queen's outfit. The pale blue coat and hat she wears in Dunedin have already been seen before. During a visit to the Elphin Showground in the City Park at Launceston, Tasmania, only eight days earlier, she wore exactly the same outfit.

My aunt has filled the sky with cloud. Now she is deciding on the first pieces of blue.

One of the sheep butted me, she says. Just as I was taking aim. I ended up pulling the trigger far too soon. I just swung around and hit it in the head. It wasn't part of any grand design.

You had better give me the gun, I say. We'll have to get rid of it.

What gun? says my aunt. You're a dear boy, Priam, but I haven't got the faintest idea what you're talking about.

I explain to the others in the creative writing workshop that my great-grandfather simply pushed his way into the story.

'I didn't mean him to play much part at all. He just got bigger and bigger.'

'I wonder if you could use him somewhere else,' says Tom. 'See, perhaps you've really got several stories here.'

Jane says that, as a character, she likes the great-grandfather more than the aunt.

'Are they both true, or did you make them up?'

I explain that my great-grandfather is based on historical fact but that the aunt is pretty much my own invention.

'I *thought* so,' says Jane.

'You meet people like that, though,' says Allen. 'She's not unlike any number of aunts really.'

'What about this Sheep-Dip idea?' says Tom. 'I had friends at Med. School and I've never heard that name. Not that I want to make realism a test of everything.'

'Oh it is,' says Sally. 'Is the name for the building I mean. I thought you read it out beautifully.'

'I made up the names for the sheep,' I say. 'They just came to me as a sort of silly idea.'

'Well it's really very striking for a first attempt,' says Fiona. 'I think you have every right to feel encouraged, Tony. The first section's almost a story in itself. That's where the most accomplished *writing* is.'

'My point exactly,' says Tom. 'It's really more than one story.'

'Well,' says Fiona. 'I think the main thing is that you *do* something with it. Send if off somewhere.'

My name is Anthony Priam Murphy. I mow the lawns below the Clock Tower and look after the university sheep. My aunt and I live together in a house in North East Valley. In the evenings she works at her jigsaw puzzles, while I puzzle over my short stories.

My aunt says I am her beautiful boy but that I am like the hedgehog who curls up in the middle of the road when traffic is approaching. She talks to me about my poor emotional posture. She puts a book on her head and walks up and down in my bedroom to show what she means.

She tucks me up and turns out the light. She says, 'Sweet dreams.'

But she does not believe in dreams.

In our creative writing workshop we have started keeping dream notebooks. We keep an exercise book by the bed; and when we wake, we write down everything we can remember. Then we try to make something out of it.

In tonight's dream my father and grandfather and great-grandfather are standing on the deck of a ship which has just docked at Port Chalmers. They look down towards me but they do not move towards the gangplank.

They know they are too late for the gold.

'Come ashore!' I call to them. 'Come ashore!'

They make no response. But surely they can hear me . . .

I begin to sing a song of welcome. The melody is beautiful. I do not understand the words but know that they are part of the beauty.

All the time that I am singing I stand absolutely still. My great-grandfather, the first Priam Murphy, dissolves. Of course. My grandfather dissolves, too.

My father hesitates, then moves towards the gangway . . .

This is a dream. At any moment I may wake. Clouds pour across the sky and my lungs fill with air as though they might be sails.

SOME QUESTIONS I AM FREQUENTLY ASKED

Q. THROUGH HERE? Are you sure? Through the wardrobe?

A. Yes, mind your head. It's quite low in there. Just push on through.

Q. Oh, I see, there's a door at the back.

A. Yes, it's like a secret entrance. It's like having to enter a *Boy's Own* adventure story before you can sit down and start writing.

Q. And you actually write through here?

A. Yes. It's private, obviously: no one bothers me. But it's also a good spot in summer, lots of sun and the big blue curtains. And then in winter it can be quite cosy. The starbelly stove makes a big difference.

Q. Do you follow a strict routine, then? Do you come through here every morning?

A. Well, I'm usually at my desk by nine each day. I write in a painstaking longhand, in exercise books bought for me by my son Pablo expressly for the purpose. I work through to about one o'clock, all things being equal, and by then Mrs Austen has prepared me a light meal of green peppers and sasque-bette.

Q. Is part of that time spent revising? Do you revise much?

A. Oh, revision is certainly important. After I have eaten a light lunch of peppers and sasquebette, Mrs Austen clears away. We chat for a while perhaps, and then usually I stroll along the clifftops, Punch comes with me, and I might stare out at the islands. Phrases occur to me, they always do, and I try to

43

remember them. I have a superstitious feeling that I must not write these phrases down at the moment they come to me, that they are not given for this purpose. Perhaps this is something that will interest your readers? Then in the evening, if the thought appeals, I make my way across the paddocks to the local hotel. Some of the regulars are real characters. Occasionally I take notes.

Q. I've read somewhere that there are quite large sasquebette plantations on some of the islands. Have you written about them? The islands, I mean?

A. Not yet, but I would like to.

Q. Have you written about the hotel? I can't recall anything. Actually, let me just play that back. It would be terrible if the batteries were flat or something, just the sort of thing that happens to me.

A. Not yet, but I would like to.

Q. Sorry about that, I just had this feeling all of a sudden that I'd better check. I see several yellow exercise books on the table over there. Does that mean you're working on something at the moment?

A. Yes. A novel.

Q. Can you say something about it?

A. I don't think I wish to talk about it, because that might be to take the whole enterprise for granted. One of the great rules in this business is, never discuss work in progress.

Q. Oh well . . .

A. But I can read you a little. Here is how it starts:

> The coup leader calls around. There is a small evening breeze, it shakes the bamboo at the bottom of the garden. Birds cling there — at the centre of the grove, hidden from view, they sleep and sway.

It is hard to go on thinking of him as Malcolm. It is strange how the uniform makes a difference.

He has brought me a Dennis Wheatley novel: *The Devil Rides Out*. It sits on the table between us.

'What would it be?' he says. 'Twenty years?'

The book has my name in it. The handwriting is mine. Malcolm says he borrowed it when we were both at school together.

We sit on the verandah and watch the stars above the bamboo, the southern constellations. We talk about Monsoon Asia with Bully Ferguson, the coloured chalk maps he made on the blackboard. Classmates. Far-off days. Have I seen anything of Gary and Jim? Do I know how they are doing? Tom is in Hamilton, still pulling teeth, have we kept in touch? And so on and so on and so on. Then —

'We need you, Philip.'

My fame as newsreader. As a media personality.

'If it would make things easier, think of it as a personal favour — old times sort of thing.'

My skills with the autocue. My knowledge of current affairs. My reassuring manner. My air of quiet authority. My Liberty tie.

'You have a way of reading the news,' says Malcolm, 'I don't know how you do it but you do, so that every single viewer feels *included*. Did you know that?'

I say nothing. He makes a mark on his clipboard.

He offers me Antarctica, sections of Australia, mistresses with great smooth marbly limbs . . .

Or am I imagining this?

I agree to think it over. We walk down to the gate together.

The woman next door is out on the footpath, calling the name of her dog. *Fairburn! Fairburn!*

Men stand at attention, they salute Malcolm as he

climbs into the waiting limousine. The stars above.
The southern constellations.

Malcolm drives away beneath an evening moon.

That's just short of an A4 page, single spacing. I'm not sure about the present tense, now that I read the thing out loud. It sounds a bit mannered, perhaps. How does it come across to you?

Q. Fine; it's really good.

A. I hope you're not just saying that.

Q. No, I really thought it was excellent. Actually it's the names in there that fascinate me. Why do you use names like Malcolm and Philip?

A. Well, why anything, I suppose. They're just names, it isn't something I've thought about a great deal, I must say . . .

Q. It's just that they seem so *ordinary*, the names themselves. And I don't think of your *writing* as ordinary. So I thought it must be deliberate.

A. Well, probably not for me to say — though I don't wish to reject your observation out of hand. But Fairburn, for what it's worth, turns out to be the absolutely crucial character in there.

Q. The dog?

A. Yes.

Q. Fascinating. Do you have a dog yourself?

A. I used to have one, but alas I shot it by accident a few months ago — I was firing at an intruder. So that was the end of Michelle. I haven't had the heart to replace her. Still, I winged the intruder, I'm pleased to say.

Q. Right . . . let me just look at this list of questions here . . . Ah yes, do you have a favourite work?

A. Of my own?

Q. Yes.

A. I think that *Banks* is probably the most *successful* thing I've done. There was the film and so forth.

Q. That's the novel about Sir Joseph Banks and his 10 servants?

A. Yes.

Q. The thing I like about it is the way you have the 10 chapters, you know, with each one being from the point of view of one of the 10 servants. But Banks himself isn't even *named* in the text, is he?

A. No.

Q. I think it's really clever, the way that works.

Q. Well, you're very kind. They turned it into cheap costume drama, the film people: sex and sailing ships. But I can't say that it *interests* me very much any more. The thing I like best is a little poem called 'Murihiku Wagon Music', which *Landfall* rejected, did you know, years ago. Now they beg me to send them things, of course.

Q. Would you like to be Maori?

A. Pardon?

Q. Would you like to be Maori? It's a question I'm asking every writer, well all the Pakeha writers. The Maori writers, the ones who'll talk to me, I ask them if they'd like to be Pakeha. I get some interesting responses.

A. Well I actually have a little Maori blood . . .

Q. But how do you *identify?* That's the real issue.

A. On days that are merely overcast, I think of myself as Maori. But when it rains I am Pakeha, soaked to the skin.

Q. That's it? That's what you're going to say?

A. That will have to do. I shall have to disappoint you. I used to be all for the joys of simple sunbathing, of course, back in the days when we still had an ozone layer.

Q. Fair enough. But what's your *location*. As a person. Imaginatively speaking. I know you travel, I know you speak a lot of languages. Do you think of yourself as a specifically New Zealand writer?

A. Ah, that is a question I am frequently asked, and here is my answer, which is a little oblique and takes the form, more or less, of a letter. Someone is being addressed but you will have to imagine this person. This time, no names.
    Beloved!
    I'm sorry!
    I forgot that we were engaged to be married
    I forgot that just for a while there
we were seeing something of each other. Yes I got drunk and played around, well of course. Yet just for a while there it was all courtship phase, we were on a ship's deck, singing our way to land, we courted each other word by word, we went up or down the charts, I don't remember. You stood and I stood: we gazed at one another across the sitting and kneeling members of the gamelan orchestra, the farmyard full of dark, metallic birds, a pair of shadow puppets who watched the quality of the light, who waited for the light to fade, mere tourists struggling with the view, and people put their hands together in the usual fashion, there was applause, I remember it well, and that was the very moment that I fell in love.
    But what about you?

Q. Me? How do you mean?

A. No, not *you*. Not in this tiny narrative sequence. This is still the letter.

Q. Oh, sorry.

A. I'll continue.

Q. Yes. I'm really sorry.

A. Then, just last week, long after you were gone, long after you were gone, I heard a repeat broadcast of your 10-minute radio talk on the current state of New Zealand English. There was your voice again, it spoke of tag phrases and commas, it discoursed upon its own rising inflections. Did we really speak like that? But you were my beloved, you were supposed to treat me well, where were you? Late at night I listened to the silence in the radio, the noise of rain after the station closes down. Where were you? Then I went to an old friend's funeral, and at the crematorium, cream and gold, after a few sad words, they played both sides of *Astral Weeks*. Beloved, oh beloved, those are the sort of people I used to go around with. The living feel rejected by the dead — not so much left behind as pushed away. That is something I have come to think. As for *Astral Weeks*, the truth is that some of it lasts and some of it doesn't.

There we are.

Q. Pardon?

A. That's it. I've finished the letter. The answer to your question.

Q. I have to admit I haven't taken it all in. It's very *rich*. Were you inventing it as you went along, or is it a thing you do by heart?

A. Oh. I extemporise each time. But you can use your machine to play it back later, you'll find it makes some sort of sense.

Q. Well, it's an astonishing view from up here.

A. Yes, on a clear day you can see the outer islands. There's a tree on one of them — Little Tartan or Big Tartan, I don't know which — and people say that if you climb it in the right weather conditions, after 24 hours of rain is one of the important elements, I seem to remember, you can see Australia.

Q. Australia. Really?

A. I don't know if you saw a man with a rifle in the gardens as you came up?

Q. Yes. He stared at me . . .

A. Well that would have been my brother-in-law, Punch. He's a useful fellow. Anyway, it was Punch who planted the tree — about 10 years ago. It's just a young South Island rata. But the thing is, it was Punch who started the story, he put it around quite deliberately. And now it has a life of its own. It just goes to show. Of course, people are very gullible.

Q. This is probably a rather obvious question, but did you always want to be a writer?

A. I don't ever remember making a conscious decision. The rainy days came and went. But I don't remember a time when I thought I would be anything else. I wrote the usual little tales and rhymes when I was a child.

Q. Did you have a happy childhood?

A. Oh yes. Certainly as a young child, until I was 10. But then things changed.

Q. Changed? How do you mean?

A. My mother lay seriously ill. She sat up in bed at the transplant hospital, her hands crossed over her breasts. She rocked a little. Weakness, weakness: she needed a new heart. Photographers came and went. There was the public appeal, you see. She gave a wan smile at appropriate moments.

My father drove to the hospital. He had made a list of cheerful things to say. He was a gloomy man in his early forties, hair already grey yet plenty of it, and he rehearsed his list of cheerful things as he turned right into Murihiku Road, not particularly looking to see what was coming. His last words were: 'new vacuum cleaner'.

Q. New vacuum cleaner?

A. Yes, he was planning to buy one. I was in the back seat with my two sisters. None of us were hurt. I think Glenys had bruised ribs, something like that.

Q. Your father died, then . . .

A. My mother lay waiting at the transplant hospital, wondering if there was some delay. Meanwhile the organ transplant unit took my father's heart to the hospital, they opened my mother's chest, sawing through the bone with a small handsaw which is kept expressly for this purpose. They wedged her ribs open, a breast on each side of her body, and they removed her heart and replaced it with my father's. The operation took six hours, and two days later she was sitting up in bed drinking a cup of tea.

Q. Amazing. I don't think you've written about any of this . . .

A. She came home for Christmas dinner. The newspapers carried photographs of her in a party hat: mother opening a box of chocolates, mother pulling a cracker, mother smiling broadly. Then she started to slip. They can do a lot more than they used to, but eventually everyone starts to slip. My sisters and I sat at her hospital bedside, intensive care, she was singing her way to shore, her skin was golden, jaundiced, and the bottles above her bed filled slowly with yellow phlegm, they were draining her lungs as part of their attempt to manage her condition. It was essentially a management problem. My sisters and I sat and watched her. The look on her face! I have spent my life trying to describe it. She was rejecting my father's heart.

The doctors issued a press release which said she had died of 'uncontrollable rejection'. There was a big funeral service, lots of people from the press and radio and television, and even a representative of the then Minister of Health, who made himself known to us afterwards. Of course, this was in the days when we still had a Minister of Health.

Q. So you were made an orphan at the age of 10. Your sisters, too.

A. Yes. The way I think of it now, we were the victims of

uncontrollable rejection. For years after that, I went to my room straight after tea and slammed the door. My aunt thought I was crying, but I was singing. I was listening to the radio, I was learning the songs of uncontrollable rejection. All those sad songs you sing along to, all that obvious music. The golden oldies. The blasts from the past . . .

Q. Well, I don't know what to ask you next . . .

A. Come and look at this, then.

Q. I've actually got lots of other questions.

A. But come and look all the same.

Q. The poster on the wall? I was wondering actually, earlier on . . . all the diagrams and things.

A. The whole thing is a kind of prophetic chart, it tells the future. It's something Napoleon used to consult, or so they say.

Q. That's why his picture's there! I was wondering.

A. Yes. There's a whole set of questions, you can probably see, and the idea is you ask a question and then work out which answer applies to you. Would you like to try?

Q. Well, yes, if you're sure . . . It sounds interesting.

A. All right, make 5 rows of dashes, if you would please, on this sheet of paper — roughly 12 marks to a row, but don't consciously try to count to 12 or anything. All right? Here, use this pencil.

Q. Like this? Is this right?

A. Yes, that's it. Okay, and now I can work out that your code mark looks . . . like this . . . and now all you have to do is cast your eye over the questions and choose one you'd like to ask.

Q. This column here?

A. Yes, any of those.

Q. All right. Let's see . . . Will my name be immortalised, and will posterity applaud it? Shall I ever recover from my present misfortunes? Are absent friends in good health, and what is their present employment? Shall I ever find a treasure?

A. Sorry, I thought I said at the start: you can only have one question.

Q. Oh, I realise that, I'm just deciding. Thinking aloud. All right . . . Shall I be successful in my present undertaking?

A. That's your question?

Q. Yes. Shall I be successful in my present undertaking?

A. Hang on then . . . let's look . . .

This is a question I am frequently asked, and here is my answer: 'Examine thyself strictly, oh luckless wight, whether thou oughtest not to abandon thy present intentions. For thou shalt be turned away, and never know it.'

Q. Well!

A. Sometimes it can be a bit discouraging.

Q. What does wight mean?

A. I believe it's an old fashioned way of saying person.

Q. Oh . . . All right, then. Does the person whom I love, love and regard me?

A. Just one question, remember?

Q. Sorry, I forgot. Well, I'd better ask you a few more questions before the tape runs out.

A. Fine. Off you go.

Q. Do you revise a lot?

A. Not really.

Q. Do you have a favourite piece of work?

A. Always the piece I'm currently working on.

Q. Do you read reviews of your work?

A. Hardly ever.

Q. What happens to Philip?

A. Pardon?

Q. Philip, in your new novel.

A. I wish I could tell you. But I mentioned earlier, I have a policy about work in progress.

Q. Sorry. I was forgetting . . .

A. Oh, turn that thing off a minute then.

Q. The tape recorder?

A. Yes.

Q. Okay, it's going again. That's fascinating. The Ministry of Rain idea. Do you think Philip *deserves* to have all that happen to him, though?

A. Well, Philip says: 'I'm sorry, Malcolm, I'm going to have to say no.' And Malcolm says: 'You're saying no?' And Philip says: 'Yes, I'm going to have to say no.'

Q. End of Philip.

A. You could say that.

Q. He's certainly a very tedious character.

A. Pardon?

Q. I said, do you get many visitors here?

A. People turn up. I usually turn them away.

Q. Do you believe we are put on this earth for a purpose?

A. Sorry?

Q. Do you believe we are put on this . . . Look, what are you doing now?

A. Sorry?

Q. What are you doing now? With that thing?

A. I am coming towards you in a threatening manner — the manner I adopt when confronting intruders.

Q. Why? Look . . . Stay away from me!

A. It's all right, calm down. Just my little joke. That is how I turn away unwanted visitors. It works rather well.

Q. Oh.

A. But you will have gathered that I am tired, we must bring this discussion to an end. My son Pablo will be waiting to see you to the door. Punch will be waiting to see you to the gate. And I expect your editor will be waiting for you to return with all this splendid material you must have.

Q. I'm sorry, I thought you were serious.

A. I wasn't.

Q. No.

A. Well, time to be going back through the wardrobe.

Q. Funny, I can't actually see where it is. Whereabouts did we come in?

A. Do you see that tall black painting, the one on the sheet of corrugated iron?

Q. Over there? Yes. Isn't that a painting by . . .

A. Yes, that's the one. Well, that painting masks the door through to the wardrobe.

Q. Really! That's ingenious.

A. Punch rigged it up, he's a clever fellow.

Q. One last question. Do you have any tips for aspiring writers?

A. Don't be put off by the first few rejection slips. They're part of the normal way of things.

Q. One last question.

A. Yes?

Q. What do you think of these starbelly stoves? Has yours worked out all right?

A. That is a question I am frequently asked, and here is my answer: They save space, give out a great deal of heat, and are extremely fuel efficient.

Q. That's good to know. I've been thinking of getting one, but it's quite an outlay, and you hear all sorts of conflicting reports.

A. Well, I will say one word to you. Fuel. You have to get the length of the logs exactly right. I like to saw my own. Each autumn I have a truckload of wood dumped down at the bottom of the garden, just behind the bamboo grove.

Q. So you saw the timber up yourself?

A. Indeed. Why, Punch and I were working down there earlier in the day, before you arrived. I was quietly working the handsaw back and forth when suddenly a weta fell to the ground — in two neat pieces. Sad, ugly, damaged creature.

Q. Ugh!

A. I had sawn it in half somehow. The two bits lay there for a moment. Then the head ran furiously from the body, scuttled away under the woodpile. But the body . . . the body stayed quite still, didn't budge — as if it knew there was absolutely no point in trying to give chase. That made me feel odd . . . I had to sit down . . .

Q. Uncontrollable rejection!

A. Sorry?

Q. The bit of body that was left behind . . .

A. Yes?

Q. It was suffering from uncontrollable rejection.

A. Yes . . .

Q. Your old friend!

A. Yes. Probably. Now, if you think you might need a photograph, ask Mrs Austen on the way out, and she can let you have something from the box.

Q. Thank you. Just one last question.

A. Yes.

Q. Will you sign this for me?

A. This?

Q. Yes.

A. This?

Q. Yes.

A. No.

1.

TWO DAYS BEFORE he left New Zealand Allen received a phone call. It was a woman, but not a voice he recognised.

'I hope it's not too late at night,' said the caller, 'and this is probably a mistake but I've been trying to get up courage all evening.'

It was 10 o'clock.

'Are you there?' she said.

'Yes,' he said. 'Who is this?' It occurred to him that this was how Americans talked, that he was acting.

'Oh, I'm *very* sorry. I think perhaps I've made a mistake.'

'Pardon?' said Allen.

'You're not the Samaritans, are you?'

'This is a private number. Was it the Samaritans you were trying to call?'

'I feel extremely silly,' said the woman. 'It's taken me a week to get to the point, and then I get a wrong number.'

She had an educated voice, a speech lessons voice.

'It's all right,' he said.

'Actually I've found out I'm dying,' the woman said. 'It's not at all fair for me to be telling you this, I realise that. But I had it all worked out. I was going to say it right away when they answered.'

Allen made a noise. A shrugging noise in his throat.

'Is your number quite near theirs? I suppose you get a lot of calls like this.'

'No,' he said. 'It hasn't happened before.'

'I've been sitting here looking at photographs. It's silly. I had them all in a shoebox.'

For some reason Allen thought of his passport photograph. He had had a new one taken a couple of months earlier, colour, yet somehow it looked pale and dated.

'It has one of those polysyllabic names,' said the woman. 'I suppose you'd like me to hang up?'

'No,' he said. 'It's all right. It really is.'

'You've got a lovely voice, did you know that? It seems a shame to let you go.' The woman paused. 'Are those children I can hear in the background?'

'I don't think so.' The kids were in bed. 'It might be a bad line.'

'I'm finding it quite hard to hear you,' said the woman. 'Would you mind holding on a minute? I'll get the children to turn the radio down.'

He waited, pressing the receiver hard against his ear. Could he hear a radio in the distance? Children's voices? People quarrelling? He could not tell.

From time to time Jean came through to the hall with an inquiring look on her face. He waved her away. Once she pointed to her watch.

He held on for 14 minutes, waiting for the dying woman to return. Then he hung up.

2.

London was cold — grey and puzzling. People bumped into one another on the footpaths, they clustered in shivering groups around map-books. Black rubbish bags were stacked against shopfronts, taxis nudged their way along the streets. He had found a small hotel a few blocks from the British Museum. His room was on the top floor, with a view of roofs and chimney pots. Mary Poppins stuff.

The roof of the building opposite was buried in rubble — timber, plasterboard, lumps of plumbing and splintered brick. Men lowered it all through scaffolding to a skip below. A sign on the front of the building said *Prestige Office Space*. Along the road another sign said *Superior Office Space*.

His first act had been to get out the South Pacific board. He put New Zealand in place, in the picture, then propped the game on top of the dressing table. Evidence of home. On the calendar above his bed he circled the departure date — making sure he was sure of it. There was something wrong with the calendar. The legend read, 'March — the Gardens at Crathes Castle, Grampian'. But the picture was of Ben Nevis, snow-clad, against a background of cloud.

He woke with a start at three in the morning. In the thin light from the bedlamp he searched for the book Jean had given him. *The Envoy from Mirror City*. It was part of the life story of Janet Frame, the New Zealand writer. It was about the time she had spent overseas — a suitable gift for travellers.

He leafed through the pages. Janet Frame was in Andorra, in the Pyrenees. She had become engaged to an Italian, El Vici Mario, who lodged in the same house as she did. They had walked together in the mountains, and he had said to her, *'Voulez-vous me marier, moi?'* El Vici could speak three languages. He had a blue-and-white bicycle, picked grapes and had fought against the fascists. Janet Frame did not say yes but she did not say no either. She did not know how to. She told El Vici that she had to go to London before the marriage, that there were 'things to see to'. She would be back soon. She bought a return ticket — but she never meant to return.

Allen marked his place; he yawned.

Deep in Andorra, deep in Allen's sleep, El Vici waited patiently for Janet Frame. He whispered to himself in French, Spanish and Italian. He was a tall, stooped figure with two-toned shoes, and he wheeled his blue-and-white bicycle along the roads of Europe, road after road, until one day, there he was, wheeling his bicycle through the small arcade behind New Zealand House. El Vici gazed into the window of Whitcoulls' little bookshop. He saw a display of books by Janet Frame. He shivered in the cold.

Allen had just finished serving a customer when El Vici pushed open the shop door.

'Prego,' said El Vici. He was holding the South Pacific board. *'Dov'è Nuova Zelanda?'*

El Vici's nicotine-stained finger hovered above the expanse of blue. Allen felt sorry for him. Another traveller lost in a foreign city.

He took El Vici's finger and dipped it in a jar of Vegemite.

'Taste that,' he said. 'Go on, try it.'

3.

A man in the trade section at New Zealand House said to him across a desk that he should really have made some sort of preliminary appointment before he left home. He seemed pleased to be talking, though. He introduced himself as Mike Bekeris. He drummed his fingers on the game board.

'Lots of blue,' he said. 'South Pacific, eh?'

'Well, the real game mostly takes place in the players' consultations and so on.' Allen felt he had to offer something. 'It's a role-playing game, really. The board's as much a matter of focus as anything. Every time you discover a new country you can place it on the board, physically put it there. So while you have to work with given names, you can build up the map as you go along. We've tried to mimic the actual conditions of exploration. In fact, you could play a whole game through without even discovering New Zealand.'

A girl put her head around the door and said, 'That's all right about Martin Crowe.'

Mike Bekeris said to Allen: 'Not quite my sort of thing, personally, board games. But then your problem isn't going to be selling it to me.'

'No,' said Allen.

'I'll be straight with you, Mr Douglas.' Mike Bekeris leant across the desk like an actor in a play. 'A lot of people come in here in your position — cottage industry sort of thing — and there isn't a great deal of return for anyone on the time put in. In any case, my hands are tied. I can give you, oh, half an hour, but then you have to decide just how serious you want our involvement to be.'

'Fair enough,' said Allen.

'Now I take it you aren't in production yet — well you can't be, or you'd have something more finished to show me. So what are your options? I'd say you can try and market direct, or you can pass the whole thing across to one of the big companies.'

'How do you mean?'

'Well, you would license Waddingtons, let us say, to produce and market the game in certain territories. I won't be telling you anything new there. Your problem is that Waddingtons might not see much future for a game like this in Europe or North America; and they might want to sell back into Australasia. If they want to see you at all.'

'We thought we would try to do our own marketing at home,' said Allen.

'So: direct marketing. But remember that over here you'd be chasing your tail inside a huge market looking for the specialist market. You'd certainly need someone on the ground, so you'd be looking at a fairly big outlay in the first instance. So maybe that means you have to go after sponsorship.'

'You mean here?' said Allen. 'Or at home?'

'Actually, the thing you have to decide,' said Mike Bekeris, 'is whether you want us to come any further down the track with you. We've moved on to a firm cost-recovery system these days: I don't come free on the tax-payer. So if you'd like us to do a bit of preliminary work — e.g. try to set up appointments with game manufacturers — then you have to commit yourself to a bit of expenditure. However you go, you can still write off 60 percent of your trip as product development.'

Allen stared at a wall poster — 'Auckland: City of Sails'. The blue slashed with sheets of white. He felt that Mike Bekeris was daring him to do something quite outrageous. But what, exactly?

'Why don't you think about it,' said Mike Bekeris, 'and give me a call over the next few days?'

The cold ate into everything. Sheets of paper flapped slowly down the Haymarket. Allen walked up through Soho, past restaurants and sex shops. It was mid-afternoon, a respectable time of day, and Soho seemed more discreet, more muted than he remembered. There were no posters outside the cinemas he passed. No one called softly from the mouths of hostess bars.

Sex was more prominent in the Virgin Games Shop in Oxford Street. At least, he found himself noticing the sex games first. Libido, Foreplay, Dr Ruth's Game of Good Sex. They seemed to be versions of strip poker, overlaid with questions of the Trivial Pursuit kind. Dr Ruth promised 'interactive cards'.

The fantasy games bred among themselves at the back of the shop. Dungeons and Dragons, Talisman, Runequest, Call of Cthulhu, Thieves' World, Star Trek, Sorcerer's Cave . . . Near them were the history games. You could fight every campaign of the American Civil War, you could join battle with Napoleon across the map of Europe. Among the World War II games, one called Pacific War caught his eye. But it turned out to involve America and Japan fighting the battles of 1941–45.

He asked an assistant if the shop had any travel or exploration games and was pointed to a display of a game called Capital Adventure — 'a travel game for people going places'. Some skill seemed to be involved in choosing the best air route between one capital city and the next. 'Take calculated risks,' said the box, 'and face the dangers that every global traveller meets.'

But there was no overlap with South Pacific.

He looked for the assistant again and described South Pacific, pretending it was a game he had read about somewhere and would be interested to buy.

'Sounds interesting,' said the assistant. It was the sort of thing they would want to have in stock, but he had never seen it. Did Allen know who made it?

'A New Zealand company, I think.'

'Ah, well.'

'If I get the details,' said Allen, 'I could drop you a note.'

'We'd surely appreciate it. We try to be comprehensive. I *think* there used to be something called Columbus. Discover America sort of thing.'

Back at the hotel Allen pushed open the door of the tiny guest lounge. A wall heater beamed its warmth on a Bengali family who sat in front of the television. One of them, an elderly woman, held a badminton racquet across her knees. Allen watched for a few minutes — Tottenham and Arsenal in extra time — then went up to his room.

His bed had been made, the cover turned back. Two hairclips lay on the pillow. He stared at them, at the shiny insect legs. He felt for his wallet in his pocket.

He looked out Monika's number and went down to the coin-box in the hall. She answered the telephone herself. She had been expecting to hear, she said. Jean had sent a letter: they must get together.

'I'm afraid it wouldn't work for you to come round here,' she said. 'But I wonder if we mightn't do something on Saturday? I can bring Lark. We can make a bit of a day of it. The thing is, I haven't got all that much money at the moment.'

4.

They met under an AIDS billboard outside the London Dungeon. Allen insisted on buying the tickets. Lark was half-price, in any case.

'I'll write you off as a business expense,' he said.

'I hope you don't mind starting off here,' Monika said as they walked through the clinical half darkness. 'Lark's been wanting to come for ages. I'm sure it'll be dreadful. Like the Chamber of Horrors.'

She had a green jewelled stud in the side of her nose. It glinted, catching the candlelight as they moved around.

'Are we under the river?' asked Lark. 'Bet we are.' She ran ahead.

They strolled among the unconvincing horrors of tourist London, passing from a scene of Druid sacrifice to a life-size model of St George, who was strapped to an X-shaped cross and bled where his flesh had been scraped by jagged combs. Further on, blood poured from the neck of Mary Queen of Scots like water from a playground drinking fountain. Behind a window live rats scurried about a skull.

'Poor things,' said Lark. 'Aren't they cute?'

'It's a *plague* display,' said Allen. 'You're supposed to be frightened.'

Beside the skull was a bowl filled with grain. He could just make out the lettering of the word DOG on the bowl's surface.

They paused in front of Sawney Beane, the Scottish cannibal. He and his family had lived for 25 years in a cave near Edinburgh. They killed unsuspecting passers-by, cutting up their bodies and pickling them. They chuckled horribly over their evening meal. After they had been captured, the men were castrated; their arms and feet were cut off, and they were left to bleed to death. The notice said that the women 'were burned in three fires'.

'Why?' said Lark. 'Why did they do that to the women?'

'Witch paranoia,' said Monika. 'They thought the women had all the real power.'

'Your father would know,' said a woman, tugging a small boy after her. But she was talking about something else.

They sat in a cafeteria at the Barbican.

'I thought it would be *frightening*,' said Lark.

Monika fingered the bone pendant which Allen had brought her from Jean.

'It's designed not to be,' said Monika. 'You're supposed to get a taste of terror but without the reality.'

She looked at Allen as if to indicate that she was saying one thing to Lark and another to him.

'Listen,' said Lark. She read out a witch's spell from one of the postcards Allen had bought.

'To win the love of a woman who does not want you, thread a needle with her hair and run it through the fleshiest limb of a dead man.'

She looked at her mother's cropped hair.

'You're safe, Mummy. No one would ever get your hair through the needle. It's far too short.'

'First find your dead man,' said Monika. 'Then we'll see.'

Allen remembered her taking his hand in a Greek restaurant in Camden Town, years ago. She had long hair then. Jean was there. His fingers were clenched up inside his palm. She unbent his fingers, one by one, then placed his hand flat, palm down, on the table. 'That's advice,' she said, 'not a proposition.'

'I think you should send your children the scariest ones,' said Lark.

Outside it was snowing. The snow fell into a long rectangular pond of water. There were ducks on the water, and beyond it was the 16th-century church of St Giles-without-Cripplegate where, said the guidebook, Oliver Cromwell had been married.

Lark went out to stand in the snow. She waved at them through the window. But the snow wasn't going to settle.

'Eight years old,' said Allen. 'Amazing.'

'Jean hasn't seen her since she was five weeks old.'

Lark waved through the window.

'But she had to go back,' said Allen. 'We went back together. She'll be across on the next trip. If this game works out.'

'South Pacific,' said Monika.

'South Pacific,' said Allen.

A pale leaflet lay on the floor outside his bedroom door.

'Rubber: the fantasy; Love Potions; Pillow Talk; The Mistress: I'm waiting to talk to you!' There were drawings of girls in lingerie, and a list of names, each with a telephone number. *Saucy Girls!*

He folded the sheet and tucked it into his pocket. A souvenir.

Next day, Sunday, he walked in the City, drifting through anaemic sunshine. At St Paul's he bought a tiny crystal bell for Jean. There was a giftshop just inside the main entrance.

In his hotel bedroom he played a game of South Pacific. But his mind failed to concentrate. Player A discovered Samoa but failed to control his crew, who introduced the native population to alcohol, then a few moves later gave them syphilis. Player B drifted in the blue.

Allen lay on the bed and masturbated. He would not call Mike Bekeris.

He tried to imagine the voice of a saucy girl but could only imagine silence. But it was all right. The light caught the jewel in the side of Monika's nose as she lowered her head towards him, and her hair, long, abundant, fell forward, shielding her face.

5.

He spent his last two days staying with one of his father's cousins, Margaret. Margaret's house lay directly beneath the flight-path at Gatwick. She could tell one kind of aircraft from another by the engine noise as they came in to land. On top of the television she kept a photograph of her late husband.

It was an amiable duty visit. Allen gave news of home, and Margaret was happy to leave him largely to himself. He went for walks, jotted down notes for a possible game on Antarctic exploration, glanced at a chapter from the Janet Frame book. He would leave the book with Margaret.

There was news of a ferry disaster. A boat had capsized sailing out of a Belgian harbour. As many as 200 were feared drowned. Margaret settled in her chair in front of the television, holding the remote control, flicking between channels.

Allen rang a saucy girl. He pressed the phone close to his ear.

A voice welcomed him to International Celebrity Line. He was through to Erica Croft.

Erica Croft explained that as a top model she visited many exciting places. Today she was on location in the South Pacific.

'We're shooting one of those chocolate bar commercials — you know, the desert island bit where you discover the treasure chest full of chewy bars. It's lovely out here, with the bleached golden sands and palm trees and gently rippling waves.'

She said that since they had a break in shooting, she would say something about some of the other countries she had been to.

'Once I went to shoot a calendar with a few other girls in North Africa. We were hoping to get a lovely tan and come back with great stories and lovely pictures, but the whole trip was an absolute disaster. There were sandstorms on the beach and it poured with rain. All the girls got bitten by insects.

'Another trip I went on earlier this year was to Cyprus, to shoot a commercial for babies' nappies. There were 25 babies plus all the

67

parents plus all the lighting plus the cameraman — all in one tiny room which was actually a ballet school. Well you can imagine the chaos in there. That was another trip that turned out to be a bit of a disaster. But they managed to make the commercial in the end, it came out looking ever so good.

'Before I go, let me just tell you today's secret. I'd really like to learn to fly.'

Allen pressed the receiver to his ear. 'Don't forget to call tomorrow when I'll be revealing even more about myself,' said Erica Croft. Then there was music, then the line went dead.

6.

London — Bombay — Perth — Melbourne — Auckland

He was next to a young couple. The man was Chilean; he looked like a teenager. The woman was Scottish and spoke for both of them. They were going to Australia: a new start. They played Scrabble, the husband and wife, on a small magnetic board. The man kept consulting a paperback dictionary.

Just after dawn they landed at Bombay. Transiting passengers strolled past a line of shops. Stall owners stood in their doorways with heads held sideways, squinting. The terminal building was fairly new, but it held an evening darkness. Allen was pleased when the reboarding call was made.

The plane taxied out to the end of the runway, swung laboriously about and began to gather speed. The seats next to Allen were empty. What had happened to the young couple? Through the window he could see army vehicles in the distance, painted in camouflage greens.

Then he felt himself thrown forward. The engines shrieked, the cabin shook. The overhead baggage doors flapped open, trembling like absurd wings.

Allen gripped the armrests. The plane was braking, skidding. He could see other passengers hunched forward, arms shielding their heads in what, it half dawned on him, was the recommended crash position.

The plane bumped off the runway, lurched to a halt. The engines stopped.

It would be a bomb. Someone was talking in a high voice towards the back of the cabin. A baby was crying.

Then the captain was speaking over the intercom. He apologised. A warning light had come up on a panel, probably nothing at all, but of course better to be safe than sorry. They wouldn't be leaving for a while now, he was afraid; it was going to be some time before the brakes cooled.

'Let me reassure you, however. There was plenty of runway out in front when I applied the brakes. But I do apologise for the rather sudden stop.'

The plane limped across to a remote corner of the airfield. An army vehicle kept it company. Beyond the tarmac there was a kind of shantytown. Faces stared through a perimeter fence.

People talked. The cabin crew brought drinks. An hour later the captain made a further announcement. Several tyres had blown out during the braking operation. A hunt was on for replacements, which were proving hard to find. He was going across to airport control to talk to London just to see if regulations might not be stretched a little — not, of course, beyond the bounds of passenger safety.

Much later, it seemed, an airline official came on board to announce that passengers were now able to proceed to the terminal. But of course they might stay aboard the carrier if they wished. This would be the only chance to disembark, however, and departure might still be several hours. He wanted to remind passengers that the terminal was air-conditioned.

About two-thirds of the cabin filed out to the waiting coaches. Allen remained in his seat. The plane was real, the terminal a dark imaginary place. The exit doors had been opened so that a breeze might circulate in the cabin. But there was no breeze; it was hot beyond belief, the deep insistent heat of early afternoon.

Allen made his way to the front of the plane and looked out the door. At the foot of the steps were several armed soldiers.

A few passengers stood halfway down the steps. They craned

their necks to catch sight of the wheels of the 747. An Indian passenger stood at the top of the steps.

'Nothing doing,' he said. 'You can go to the bottom step, but if your foot should touch the tarmac, then I believe these men may shoot you.'

He introduced himself. He was Mr Murugesar. 'My wife is back there,' he said. 'Keeping to her seat.'

Mr Murugesar lived in Sydney. He was an importer. 'Things of all kinds.' His wife had many relations in Bombay. These were the people they had been visiting. 'But they are hopeless people. They will never get away.' Mr Murugesar gestured towards the invisible city, apparently including all of its citizens in the sweep of his arm.

Allen could hear a flight steward explaining that permission had come through to use Air India tyres. There was only a small difference in specifications. But it would still be some time before they could begin removing the damaged ones: they were still too hot.

Mr Murugesar sat beside Allen and spoke to him of New Zealand. One day he hoped to go there. 'All of the South Pacific,' he said. 'The islands and so forth.' England, of course, where Allen had been, he knew England well.

'The sounding cataract haunted me like a passion,' said Mr Murugesar. 'Little lines of sportive wood run wild. Tintern Abbey, did you visit there?'

Allen explained that he had only been to London. A marketing trip. He talked about the board game.

'Most interesting,' said Mr Murugesar. 'We are brothers of the road.' He lowered his voice and whispered to Allen that someone had said that a limousine collecting a government minister had exploded outside the airport. 'But I think you will find this is not true,' he said.

Allen stood halfway down the steps. About thirty men were gathered around the lumpy black tyres. They prodded and gesticulated, shouting at each other.

'Well at least they're making some show of getting on with it,' said a tall Australian. He said that the real problem was that the cabin crew would soon come to the end of their shift. 'So none of the current lot will be allowed to fly out of Bombay. They'll be scouring the city for a stand-by crew. Cross everything you've got.'

Mr Murugesar was also pessimistic. Nine hours had passed; soon they would all be taken into the city. He read to Allen from a guidebook, eyeing him shyly from time to time.

'From Bombay the first Indian locomotive steamed down to Thana in 1853.'

'Bombay turns out the largest number of movies in the world.'

'Bombay is a colourful racial and linguistic mosaic.'

Mr Murugesar described the Mahalakshmi Temple. 'Goddess of Prosperity. But the city owes its name to Goddess Mumbadevi.'

He flipped through the book. 'Ah! This will interest New Zealanders.'

He held the book before him in both hands.

'Aarey Milk Colony, perhaps the largest in Asia, set amidst gardens. From the Observation Pavilion on a hillock near the entrance, one can see the process of pasteurisation and bottling of milk. This is an ideal picnic spot. Cottages available.'

Mr Murugesar lowered Allen's flight tray. He placed the book gently upon it.

'Now,' he said, '*The Gateway to India*. My gift to you.'

Passengers were filing back into the cabin. A new crew moved about, crisp and pressed. The young Chilean and his Scottish wife appeared. They smiled as though nothing had happened.

Then the plane was airborne. The new captain gave a flight time to Perth, and a cruising altitude. He invited passengers to adjust their watches. The drinks trolley came. A meal came. The young couple played Scrabble. The man made the word *sailer* on the board; he held the dictionary up in front of his wife and pointed.

Allen watched the film. Robert Redford and a beautiful woman were investigating crooked art dealers in New York.

He fell asleep and then he was in Auckland, clouds and sails. But it was London, and he was walking in the City — following someone, or being followed, he could not tell. Snow fell into the

71

concrete moats of the Barbican. El Vici rode past on his bicycle, waving slowly. *'Dov'è Nuova Zelanda?'*

But the streets were deserted. He was wading through the cold and darkness of a winter afternoon.

He began to drift with the cold. It came in clouds, leaking from walls and domes, from tower blocks, from the stone of ancient churches. He felt himself dissolving, consciousness without form, blurred and indefinite. He drifted in his blood, he seeped away.

Now the damp pores of stone opened to accept him. Atom by atom, they took him in. He was mist melting into water, dampness sinking through sand. Soon no trace of him would remain.

Yet there was something which was not taken in. He could feel it — a stubborn part of himself which would not dissolve, would not budge, would not be absorbed in stone. He reached out. He touched it. He touched it gently, with his misty hand. It was his erection, which he woke to find himself holding, high above the Indian Ocean, as the 747 reduced power and began the slow descent towards Perth.

VENTRILOQUIAL

The Hermit of Peking

THE WOMAN FROM the Historic Places Trust is nervous. Her name is Sarah. She chatters on about chopsticks, MSG, hyperactive children, she has two herself, she should know. Would the magazine contemplate a piece on turn-of-the-century sawmills? Or, and granted this goes a little beyond her own area of expertise, something on the old macrocarpa windbreaks of Southland?

I spin the revolving warmer and take a little more Stir-fried Broccoli with Hoisin Sauce, perhaps just another helping of Drunken Chicken. I make a mental note to be fair. This is Sarah's first magazine lunch, and naturally enough she is trying too hard. Also, my foot is stroking her leg.

The talk comes round to racehorses. Racehorses or something similar is often the way of it. Tom Mendoza, our bloodstock correspondent, offers the thought that there are an awful lot of horses around at the moment which seem to be named after artists. Forget all those nags called Monet or Van Gogh across in Europe. What puzzles me, says Tom, is that so many of our own folk, owners and trainers, are going the same way. So are we coming of age in a cultural sense then? Or is this further evidence of the derivative nature of our way of life? Once it was Phar Lap and Cardigan Bay; now it is Woollaston, who must, incidentally, stand not a bad chance in the Caulfield Cup . . . And Rita Angus, well there you're starting to talk household names . . .

Jimmy Kwok, proprietor of this fine establishment, comes across to ask if everything is to our satisfaction. He cannot, poor man, entirely conceal his disappointment. Like others, he had expected to see Richard Hadlee at our table. Alas, Christchurch airport has been closed for two days by an unacceptable level of bird-strikes. Never mind, we have two middle-ranking Cabinet

73

Ministers, a knight from the Business Roundtable, someone from Avalon, a country-and-western singer called Hank Mushroom, and the University Vice-Chancellor, who is also a physicist of consequence. He flies around the world discoursing on a shadow universe of dark matter . . . electromagnetic whispers . . . the place where particle physics and astrophysics join hands and speak to us . . . The V-C has taken a liking to the Stewed Pork with Fermented Beancurd and Taro — just as well since no one else is keen to pursue it beyond the first mouthful and, as usual at the Hermit of Peking, there are Jimmy Kwok's feelings to bear in mind.

I ask Sarah to come back to our handsome harbourfront tower block and elaborate her ideas a little. She bites her lower lip, toys with her rice. Hank Mushroom begins to describe his trip to Nashville. The place defies description really . . .

I try to listen. But there is nothing much for us here.

Coastal Flashback

When I was a boy I thought that throwing your voice meant precisely that. The books I read were full of heroes who saved the day by cleverly throwing their voices. All right Cunningham! Drop the gun! Overpowering villains was a routine exercise, you simply distracted them first. It was not so much that you talked without moving your lips, although that must have been important. The crucial thing was to actually make your voice come from some distant object . . . a vase of flowers across the room, or a button jar beside your mother's elbow, or the ancient great-aunt who has come to stay for a while and is now asleep in the corner — her face as pale as electricity, and her whole body giving off that fishy smell which sometimes signals an electrical fault.

I show my aunt my bag of milk bottle tops. Silver, she says. Are you a good boy, Hugo?

And when Aunt wakes, she is neither rich nor married. She is in this awful house, she has been here three years now, how did that happen? A boy in the corner is putting on a coat with a strip of reflector tape on the back; he is about to go out the door and get on his bicycle and ride off down the road to wherever it is a boy like him might go at this time of night. Don't let your uncle come and get me, cries my aunt. We explain, for the umpteenth time, that he has been dead for years. But he can *materialise,* she says. Can't you *see?*

Aunt sinks back into her chair. There is that fishy smell again. Down on the beach the gang members are giving their German shepherds a run on the sand. They throw sticks for them, dash into the surf a bit, things like that. I wheel my bicycle carefully through the twilight.

Pioneer Women's Hall

First our donation at the door. The suggested amount is $25. Quite usual, Frank tells me. We are in the kitchen/dining-room of the Pioneer Women's Hall. There is a sink just to our left; a white Zip hangs above it. Are there more of us here? Why yes. There are several elderly persons, widows and widowers, none of them known to me. No familiar faces — although isn't that Josephine the Spanish dancer on her knees at the front erecting her portable wooden floor? Frank whispers that there will not, of course, be any Spanish dancing; Josephine is actually related to the medium in some way, cousins he thinks. We settle back and wait.

Domestic Interior

Charles Laughton, the young Maori novelist, rings me up at home. I am in bed with Sarah. We ran a paragraph on him in the magazine gossip column about three months ago and he has plagued us ever since. He wants something more substantial. When are you sending that reporter round, says Charles Laughton. When we have space on the schedule, I say. Well, Hugo, people want to know about me, he says, I get approached on the street, I think you should do me soon. He begins to describe a short story he is about to start work on. It is written from the point of view of a boy from the East Coast travelling in Canada in the late 19th century. The story has a working title: 'Tolaga Bay: The Days of Sail'.

Sarah begins to do something interesting to the lower part of my body while Charles Laughton goes on with his story. I sigh into the telephone. It has been a surprising few weeks. It turns out that Sarah is my neighbour, she lives just beyond the clematis and honeysuckle. She and her husband moved in about six months ago. Frank and Sarah Husband. I hadn't even noticed the departure of the previous neighbours. Frank and Sarah Husband have no children. So what Sarah said at the Hermit of Peking was a spur of the moment invention. I find this unreliability only makes her more attractive. Frank works in the Department of Social Welfare. He is happy for Sarah to lead an interesting life, even the part of it that now involves me. He watches her vanish through the honeysuckle . . . a smile hovers on his lips . . . he makes the noise of an aeroplane taking off.

Frank Husband is a ventriloquist. He talks to his dummy, Disraeli, late into the evening. Voices are raised in argument, neither of them Sarah's. Frank watches videos; he has a fine Tarzan collection. I have told Sarah how keen I am to meet him: I always wanted to be able to throw my voice when I was a boy. Maybe drinks one evening?

I make my excuses to Charles Laughton. In fact, I tell him that it sounds as if he has the makings of a whole *novel* there. I cut him off halfway through the Inuit Ceremony of Welcome.

Sixteenth Floor

The Thursday post lands on my desk, its thump shaking the tower block. Here they are, the latest issues of *Esquire, Vogue, Penthouse, Tatler, Paris Match, Watchtower, The Face, Agricultural Machinery, Spare Rib, Oomph!, Indecent Assault, Sorcerer, Mädchen, Now/Then, Ectoplasm, Soviet Weekly, Grendel's Mother, The New Yorker, Nonetheless, Health and Beauty, Contretemps, Turf Digest, Studio International*. A modest queue has formed. I pass the magazines out to appropriate members of staff. Each goes off to comb through the pages, seeking that special piece which may meet the exacting requirements of local adaptation.

I give Sarah the latest issue of *Knave* and wink at her. And how is the piece on macrocarpa windbreaks coming along, I ask our latest staff writer. Astonishingly, she replies that she needs to travel to Southland *with* the photographer, not just write secondhand captions after seeing the contacts. Can I not get that into my head? And what about the other project? She has told me several times now about Thomas Barnhill and the trees he planted at Castle Rock station to commemorate troop dispositions at Waterloo. Have I come to a decision? Maybe she is mistaken, but she thought I was the editor.

I sigh, and stare out at the squid boats in the harbour. Sarah Husband is by no means one of those workers who kneels under the boss's desk. Though of course she would probably not refuse if asked.

Meanwhile, in the large open-plan offices on the floors below, work goes on. Lists are compiled, the telephones are busy. The lunch invitations go out, the subscription copies pour in. The newest clerical assistant goes out to buy more scissors. It is all part of our ceaseless search for new ideas.

Rainbow Warrior

Cushions around a low table, same old blackboard menu. Did we really mean to invite *two* heart surgeons? I remember posting out the invitation to the immediate past-president of Federated Farmers myself. And the others all make some sort of sense — the society astrologer, Josephine from the Spanish Dancing Academy, the politician who wants to privatise the prison services, the English Department lecturer who turns out to be New Zealand contributing editor of *Now/Then*. Don't we see that one from time to time, I say. Interesting graphics, is that the one?

The man from the English Department wears a T-shirt which says 'Make Me An Offer'. He is balding and incomprehensible; he talks and his lips don't move. He is keen to work up a piece on the death of Norman Kirk. In rhetorical terms, he declares, that whole event was a discourse substitute, wasn't it? He waits for his words to sink in. But will it make a punchy 1 500-word article, front of book, with visual potential? I fear not.

Talk among our staffers, also Josephine and the astrologer, turns to Charles Laughton. He is doing well, despite his name. Does the poor man *know?* Still, the way Fletcher Challenge snapped him up as writer in residence . . . And just the other week there was that profile in the *Listener,* quite well done though hardly enough to halt the circulation slide.

Well, says the man from the English Department, he makes it clear that he is being patient: What *happens* when we create discourse?

But here is the editor of *The Dictionary of New Zealand Biography*, we rise to greet him, distinguished man with a pipe, better late than never. We pour him a bowl of muesli. Now tell me, says the society astrologer, would you for argument's sake put someone like Charles Laughton in this book of yours? The case doesn't arise, says the editor of the *DNZB*, he isn't dead yet. Then he adds, puffing serenely: We *are* thinking seriously about Kupe.

Ye gods!

Kiri Te Kanawa has called in sick, the Everly Brothers are delayed in Manila, Colin Meads and Michael Joseph Savage have failed to answer their letters. The man from the English Department puts a 10-dollar note on the table and gets to his feet. I ate very little, he says. I just picked at my salad. He looks pleased — as if we have failed some sort of test . . .

Next Tuesday the John Wayne Chophouse, then maybe the Rive Gauche or the Rumbling Frog.

Next Door

Sarah is in the master bedroom, the door closed. She has been back from the South Island a fortnight now, working and reworking her macrocarpa piece. Frank watches *Greyfriars Bobby* with the sound down. I keep him company.

You're talking, says Frank, about distant voice technique.

He makes the noise of a bath emptying; the sound seems to

come from the ceiling. He picks up the telephone. Get me Bob Hawke. Hawke comes on the line. Frank has a long chat with him about Australian foreign policy, and Hawke agrees to most of Frank's suggested initiatives — leasing Tasmania to the French, invasion of Burma, night landings on the Malvinas. I can hear Hawke's voice, as clear as day: sleek and nasal, yet metallic down the line.

Talk to you later, says Frank. Catch you Frank, says Hawke.

Sarah calls from the bedroom: Hugo! Can I ask you something?

I go through. What is it? says Sarah.

I thought you called, I say. Can I help or something?

Not me, she says, no way, I'm doing perfectly well, thank you.

Frank flicks off the video. So there are two crucial elements, he tells me. First: the gift of mimicry, either you have it or you don't. Second: breath control, with particular regard to techniques of drone and rib reserve.

He asks me to consider a diagram of the human vocal and respiratory mechanism.

I find it hard to pay attention. There is a distressed bird flying around the room. How did it get in? It hits the window, batters the glass repeatedly, drops to the floor. I can hear the feeble beating of wings on carpet. Now a car pulls up in the street. A door slams: footsteps, a woman's voice, a single piercing scream. I race to the front door and fling it open. Nothing. Black empty night.

Frank Husband comes and stands beside me. Back in the house Sarah makes faint noises of sexual arousal. Frank's teeth flash in the moonlight. The ventriloquial effect, he says.

Pioneer Women's Hall

Flickering candlelight. Darkness of the other side. The Zip floats eerily above the sink, like ectoplasm. The man in the blue cardigan writhes between two women.

I have a message for someone in this room. You go.

Mr Mikes stops writhing; he sits upright in his wooden chair.

His arms are stretched horizontally: each woman holds a wrist. They might be nurses taking his pulse. One of them is Josephine.

You go?

Frank nudges me. Wake up Hugo!

Yes, I say, my name is Hugo. The message might be for me.

What is it dear, says Josephine. She inclines her head towards Mr Mikes. Hugo is here; have you a message for him?

Aunt Beattie . . . says that . . . she has found . . . happiness. Uncle Graham is here . . . they are together . . . again. She says . . . there is now . . . and there is . . . then . . .

My Aunt Beattie? My Uncle Graham?

She's gone, says Josephine. I'm sorry.

My Aunt Beattie?

Can we have Peter now, please? says Josephine. She and the other woman seem to tighten their grip on Mr Mikes' wrists.

Here we go, Frank whispers.

I open my notebook and lean forward.

Sixteenth Floor

Occasionally even I am astonished by the magazine's success. I pinch myself to see if it is all true. Ouch! Of course I was confident at the outset. We had put a good little team together, the right mix of skills and personalities: those who like to move the ball out quickly along the line, those who prefer to make a jinking little run. We have a circulation of 90 000 copies per issue, fully audited, steadily rising. A good 10 000 more with a Royal cover story. Not bad for something launched on hope and a shoestring just 21 months ago. Not bad, as I will probably observe in our birthday editorial, for a little country at the bottom of the South Pacific.

Advertisers clamour for space; we cannot meet the demand. Nearly 1 000 copies of each issue go to overseas subscribers eager to keep up with what goes on in our corner of the world.

On my desk, the latest titles mount up: *Harper's & Queen, Business Traveller, Cycling World, Women in Management, Country Life, Moroccan Zero, New Scientist, Marauder, Time, Newsweek, Soldier of Fortune, New Left Review, Angiospore,* the *Illustrated London News,*

Rasta!, the *Wall Street Journal, Rough Trade,* the *Joseph Conrad Newsletter.* I try to sort them into some semblance of order. The clock ticks on; the queue begins to form at my door.

Bad Dream: Domestic Interior

Hugo, says Frank, meet Hugo. Frank has brought his dummy across to say hello. The dummy's eyebrows are made of black felt; the rest of his head is painted, even the hair. The mouth can move: the middle of the chin drops away when Frank operates a lever in the dummy's back.

That's a real coincidence, I say, the names being the same. But I thought his name was Disraeli . . .

You've been talking to Sarah, says Hugo. How well the two of you have lasted. But Sarah is very much out of touch now. We've been thinking of this particular name change for quite some time, haven't we Frank?

Frank nods. His mouth drops open.

Arthur Prince and Sailor Jim. Edgar Bergen and Charlie McCarthy. Peter Brough and Archie Andrews. Shari Lewis and Lamb Chop. Paul Winchall and Knucklehead Smiff. Frank Husband and Hugo.

Next Door Flashback

Frank and I are watching a video. I wonder aloud, if I will ever get to meet his ventriloquial doll. Frank says that Disraeli is shy, he likes to keep himself to himself. But I know that later tonight, after I have gone home — maybe with Sarah, more likely by myself — voices will be raised, Frank and Disraeli will discuss the day's events, maybe even discuss me.

Sarah sits through at the big kitchen table, with shots of windbreaks spread out around her. Some of them are very fine, I have to acknowledge. The movie Frank and I are watching is an old one: *Devil Doll.* It stars a ventriloquist called Vorelli whose dummy, Hugo, becomes a monster. Hugo is locked in a cage every night.

81

Most of it is farcical; very occasionally there is that authentic note of chill.

Sixteenth Floor

Yes? I look up from my notes on the Korean Peace Dam. Oh, it's you.

Sarah stands in the doorway. She has come to hand in her final assignment: a report on the medieval jousting tournament in Tauranga.

Hugo, she says, it was too good to last. You must have known it was time.

I toy with my pen. I think: Sarah, I have seen you flabbergasted, rattled, lost for words; I have seen you gasping on my oatmeal carpet.

By the time I look up from my thoughts, Sarah has slipped out, en route to her new job at Radio New Zealand. But somewhere in North Korea, the proposed Peace Dam is still on the drawing board. The plan apparently involves the construction of a giant earth dam, with a corresponding mass of water backed up behind it, in a valley near the border. The threat is silent, but real. Should the water be released, within minutes the National Assembly Building in Seoul will be drowned. Naturally, the Government of South Korea has begun to plan its own dam; it will face the North Korean dam.

They grow slowly in the mind: the two giant walls of compacted earth, each with a vast lake spreading out behind it. Perhaps there will be pleasure boats and water-skiing. And, between the two dams, lush market gardens.

I am working my way towards the magazine's birthday editorial. It is still several issues off, but it needs to be just right. So, I have a striking metaphor, one which grows in the mind; but where will it take me? East-West relations? New Zealand's own hydro-electric schemes? The general state of preparedness of Civil Defence? I want to get some bridge, too, into the magazine itself. I wonder if I could praise Charles Laughton's new play — the one now touring China, in which all the people of the whanau go about on crutches? The dazzling symbolism, the theatrical coup, needs to be acknowledged; but maybe there is some greater lesson here? Might not the young playwright's perception apply to *all* the peoples of Aotearoa/New Zealand? Etc. And then maybe some further words about a shared future — with the magazine, its happy marriage of idealism and experience etc., playing its own small part in building the nation of the future. Like the future, we hope to be around for some time yet.

My desk sags under the weight of *Cosmopolitan, Harper's Bazaar, National Geographic, Matelot, Oggi, Chiffonier, Stand Clear of the Moving Handrail, Punch, People's Friend, Elle, City Limits, Mayfair, Gibbon's Stamp Monthly, Seance, This Way Up, High Society, Junior Alchemist, The Lady, Cropdusting Monthly, Astrolabe, Leprosy Review, Badminton Today.*

After Sarah told me, I said to Frank, Frank, I'm sorry, let me know if there's anything . . .

She's not leaving me, Hugo, Frank replied. Just you.

Pioneer Women's Hall

Mr Mikes pants and moans, jerking from his shoulders. I could swear he has an erection . . . the light makes it difficult to tell. He wails and snorts, his voice makes a smothered sound.

Yes Peter, says Josephine. Is that you now, dear? Hello? Peter?

Mr Mikes pulls his arms free. He sits with his fists clenched in front of him like a boxer, sparring with the empty air.

Oh, she says, it's Daniel. Daniel, can we please have Peter?

Mr Mikes slumps in his chair. The spirits drift down the long corridor of his body. The women take up his wrists again.

Mr Mikes says: Peg.

Hello Peter, says Josephine. Can you hear me?

Mr Mikes nods; his upper body seems to force the movement out. He says: Goodness gracious me.

For a moment he slumps. Then he straightens, the women hold him. Now his voice is American. Balham, he announces, Gateway to the South!

Mr Mikes does the whole Peter Sellers sketch: word-perfect,

voice-perfect. He carves the little holes in the tops of toothbrushes. There is honey still for tea. Then he goes straight into Sellers doing Olivier doing 'A Hard Day's Night'. Each word is cold, clipped, separate.

What next? We hold our breath.

But Mr Mikes falls forward. He has plummeted from his trance, he gives off a fishy smell. The women help him from the room.

Staggering, says Frank. What do you think, Hugo?

I do not know what to think. But I am willing to be persuaded there is a feature here, if only we can get the illustrations right. I look at my notebook. I have written the words, 'Now then'.

Tandoori Heaven

Frank Sinatra has failed to show. But we were aiming high there. Hone Tuwhare has sent an apology — a terse, handwritten note, free verse, already safe in the archive. The Deputy Prime Minister is opening a Rollerdrome in Wanganui. There has been an acceptance from the Director of the SIS. But apparently he is sitting at another table.

Still, Frank Husband is here — minus Disraeli, who is unwell. Frank is angling, not very subtly, for the recently advertised job of features editor. He is sick of the Department of Social Welfare. First things first, I say to him. Let's see what you can do with the ventriloquism piece, you need some sort of track record. He nods his head but clearly isn't happy.

One of the country's top winter-sports instructors is here. So is a rather dazzling woman, Shirley, from the DSIR; she talks of this and that. Further down the table, Charles Laughton, the playwright and novelist, chats to Josephine and her medium cousin, Mr Mikes. Occasionally one of our lunch guests hoists a video camera to her shoulder; she must be one of the performance collective, Handle With Care. Plus we have the usual assortment of office staff and eager freelances. I have ordered a Sultan's Banquet (24 hours' notice), but with extra Chicken Tikka.

Our business editor, Barry Mendoza, is talking about the new

Japanese market in name copyrights. Apparently in the last few years, people with an eye to the future have been registering Western names at the Japanese Chamber of Commerce. Now, for a nominal outlay, one enterprising Tokyo businessman has ended up owning the names of over 2 000 Italian cities and rivers. Refer to Venice in Japan, says Barry, and you pay top rates. In fact, Barry goes on, it makes you wonder about the potential of Maori names; presumably they're just there for the taking. If we don't grab them, some other bugger will.

I glance anxiously at Charles Laughton. How will he react to this sort of talk? But Charles has not heard; his head is inclined towards that of the new Leader of the Opposition, who talks animatedly about the new PVC downpipe and guttering systems. His nephew has the agency for one of the better systems. It really is the end of rust, you see.

A message. The winter-sports instructor leaves suddenly. A death on the slopes; he must go at once . . .

Anyway, says Frank, I thought I would start with something on Alexander of Abonitichos and his talking serpent. Then work my way up to the present, with separate entries for people like Le Sieur Themet, favourite of the Empress Josephine; you know, the one who could laugh on one side of his face and cry on the other. And end up with Mr Mikes himself — stressing the local angle, of course, but also the return to the idea of ventriloquism as magic, real old-time belly talking.

But who *is* the ventriloquist in a case like that? I ask. In a way it's really Peter Sellers throwing his voice, isn't it, not Mr Mikes. Assuming the whole thing (I lower my voice) isn't a hoax.

Hoax? says Frank. His mouth drops open. Hoax? You wouldn't know the first thing about it.

Along the table there is talk about the left side of the brain. About the invisible universe. The change of government. The ozone layer. The All Black tour of France.

A man at a nearby table, not one of our party, begins to grow agitated. An odd noise is coming from the floor below him. It is a woman's voice: we can all recognise the faint cries of sexual arousal. The man gets to his knees, lifts the tablecloth. There is nothing there.

The noises grow louder, but now they are coming from another corner of the restaurant. People stop eating; some get to their feet. I watch Frank's lips closely. The voice makes its cries again, small fluttering noises of pleasure and distress. I catch Frank's eye and he smiles, lifting his fork in a kind of salute.

Meanwhile our circulation continues to rise, trespassers are prosecuted, life in these islands goes on pressing its case.

CANNIBALS

PART THE FIRST

WE WERE SAILING in the Pacific. Seeking out new lands: savages and treasure, sex and mineral rights, you know the sort of thing. Our weaponry very much superior to anything we might meet, the insurance company happy, the holds well stocked, all hands on deck, charts spread out on our knees, tang of sea in our nostrils.

Day after day. Uncle James reading aloud from the Bible.

The South Seas are sprinkled with numberless islands, like stars in the Milky Way. There are whole necklaces of islands, and each jewel on the chain is another paradise.

If the charts are hard to read, that is because of the wild, uncharted waters we are venturing into.

'I love you,' says the ship to the sea. 'We have always been friends, we two, and ever shall be.'

'Yes,' says the sea. 'But oftentimes, when the wind blows high and fierce, I have been greatly troubled for your safety.'

'Yes, dear sea, it is the wind, ever, ever the wind that is making dispeace between us, because it is so seldom in the same mind.'

'True, that is the worst of the wind.'

'How beautifully blue you are today, oh sea, and what tiny wavelets you wear. I never care to go back to the noisy grimy docks when I think of you as you are now.'

'And how beautiful *you* are also, oh ship. Do you know that at a distance you might be mistaken for some bright-winged sea-bird skimming along in the sunshine. But who are these on your deck, oh ship, who make such clamour?'

'They are rough diamonds — sailors, explorers, missionaries. One or two stowaways. The occasional mutineer.'

'Oh well,' says the sea, 'nothing new there, very much the usual stuff.'

You see a peak in the distance, feathery palms and so forth, and you have to admit it's a pretty good feeling.

Our ship slices through the water, breasts the wave, on it goes through the opening in the reef, the *Tia Maria* is its name, I expect I forgot to say that earlier. I am writing on my knees, which is always difficult.

Maps all over the deck. Cap'n Tooth at the helm, old seadog. Excitement mounting. We sail in silver waters beside golden sands.

This island is probably uninhabited, so we will be able to give it a name, that's always a pleasurable thing. Maybe something from the list of names that Gerald keeps in his pocket.

Yes, the island certainly looks uninhabited. Nothing stirring. Any minute now we will lower the rowing boat and men will row ashore for coconuts and just generally try to see what they can see. The rest of us might swim a bit, or maybe sketch the extinct volcano.

'We haven't used Llandudno Junction yet,' says Gerald.

General derision.

Gerald blushes, I'll say that for him, but on he goes, he is totally undeterred.

'Let's see,' he says. 'How about Seattle? Pontypridd? Crofts of Dipple?'

But hold, who are these sinister black creatures who suddenly appear upon the shore, rank upon rank of them, three abreast, uttering cries that chill the very blood in our veins? They skip and howl, they wade into the surf and shake their fists above their heads . . .

Wait a minute . . . those black cassocks . . . those cadaverous smiles . . .

The priests of Rome! Here before us!

Break out more sail! Away! Away! While yet there is breath in our bodies!

Well, that was a near thing. Touch and go there for a while. Cap'n Tooth breaks out the rum, we decide to call the island Adventure Island, because of the adventure we had there.

'And to think it was so nearly Misadventure Island!' jokes Uncle James.

Gerald scowls below deck, murderous black sharks cruise about our little ship, but our spirits are high.

Tonight I discovered a stowaway in my cabin. It happened thus. I had knelt to say my evening prayers, when my right knee encountered something strange beneath the bunk. Upon investigation, I found a boy secreted there, a sprightly lad clad in denim, who made a dash for the door, one of those absolutely futile things for I caught him easily, even I was surprised at the ease of it, and I threw him forthwith to the floor. Upon which I had my second surprise of the evening.

The young fellow's shirt had torn a little in the course of our struggle, and as I gazed down, panting and victorious, what did I see, peeping out at me, but two quite perfect female breasts . . .

Well! My stowaway is a girl!

Her name is foreign, it sounds like Meefanwee.

I make frequent overtures of friendship to Meefanwee, and gradually I believe I gain her confidence.

Meefanwee has black hair and green eyes, a really interesting combination.

I shall keep her, I shall be her protector, I shall certainly not let on to Uncle James.

The *Tia Maria* courses on through the vast Pacific. A few days ago we had the adventure with the pirates, that was at Pirate Island. And just after that there was the island where we couldn't find a place to land. It looked so beautiful and mysterious, just rising up out of the blue Pacific, but we sailed round and round it and failed to find an opening in the coral reef. The crew grew tired of our circular motions and fell to muttering among themselves, and Cap'n Tooth had to give them more rum. But at last we were able to sail on and we decided to call the island Mystery Island, because it would always remain a mystery to us.

I keep Meefanwee concealed in my cabin.

She is my little stowaway, that is what I sometimes call her, she looks up into my face trustfully.

Sweet Jesus, it is a look which brings out all the manliness of my soul!

I read to her from the Bible, I touch her private parts.

We have let Gerald name some islands. There were actually three islands together, a group of them, and it was just after the fight with the giant octopus, and of course we were feeling good about that, and we just sort of gave him carte blanche, a French phrase, it means literally white map, I don't think that had ever occurred to me before. I am afraid Gerald rather took advantage of us, and he named the islands after three former girlfriends of his, Yvonne, Sharon and Mrs Llewellyn Davies. The islands were all uninhabited, which Gerald says just makes the names even more appropriate.

Actually there were one or two natives, several of us noticed them, but they ran off when they saw us coming.

We dumped the nuclear waste on one of the islands — Sharon, I think, but I don't really remember.

Uncle James has a rather bad snakebite, which he got when he went ashore a few days ago on Mrs Llewellyn Davies. Mrs Appleby, my aunt, is fearfully worried. His leg has swollen to several times its normal size. He cannot enter his cabin, and must lie out on the deck until the swelling subsides. It is a real nuisance: crew members are always tripping over him and he is constantly having to apologise.

Today there was a message in a bottle, that sometimes happens, I didn't see it myself but someone says there was one. I helped fight off the sandalwood traders, though, that was easy enough, we just opened fire with the really big guns and let them have it. Then we

90

found some pearls, big ones, worth millions apparently, though I personally didn't do any of the diving. But I suppose the real news is the mutiny. I should probably have mentioned it a bit earlier. The crew, led by their own obscure desires, have slain good old Cap'n Tooth and set course for Valparaiso. But not before first putting us ashore on a nearby island.

Uncle James says that we must call our island Fortunate Island — 'for surely good fortune awaits us in this Pacific paradise.'

The island has a lagoon, a coral reef, coconut palms and a mysterious mountain which could be honeycombed with underground passages, it is hard to tell. The island is probably deserted, but we will have to do some proper exploring in the next few days and find a place for signalling ships from and so on.

Meefanwee is safely ashore. I am passing her off as a member of the crew.

'Uncle James,' I say, 'meet Douglas. Douglas, this is my uncle, James Appleby. Douglas was the only one of that riff-raff, mulatto crew, uncle, with spirit enough to stand by us.'

'Pleased to meet you, my boy,' says Uncle James. 'Sorry I can't get up. My leg is still playing me up a little.'

In fact, Uncle's left leg is now twice the circumference of his upper body, and very, very pustular.

'What a lovely spot this is!'

Uncle James has summoned us all together for words of encouragement. We cluster about him on the sand. He lies like a beached whale.

'Mark these coconut palms, they have borne their fruit year after year, have died, and others have sprung up in their stead; and here has this spot remained, perhaps for centuries, all ready for man to live in and enjoy.'

He pauses. You can hear the deep incessant boom of distant combers.

'Pray tell, Mr Appleby,' says my aunt, 'what are the great merits of the coconut tree?'

'Why, I'll tell you madam: in the first place, you have the wood to build a house with; then you have the bark with which you can make ropes and lines, and fishing-nets if you please; then you have the leaves for thatching your house, and also for thatching your head if you please, ho ho, for you may make good hats out of them, and baskets also; then you have the fruit which, as a nut, is good to eat, and very useful in cooking; and in the young nut is the milk, which is also very wholesome; then you have the oil to burn and the shell to makes cups of, if you haven't any; and then you can draw toddy from the tree, which is very pleasant when fresh, but will make you tipsy if it is kept too long, ho ho; and then, after that, you may turn the toddy into arrack, which is a very strong spirit. Now there is no tree which yields so many useful things to man, for it supplies him with almost everything.'

'I had no idea of that,' replies the astonished woman. And she goes off to the far end of the beach to peruse her Bible.

'The island is evidently of volcanic origin,' remarks Gerald. 'What is your opinion, William?'

Gerald is addressing me. He and Douglas and I have gone exploring. The others are building a house back at Castaway Bay.

'But remember the reef is coral,' I say. 'Though I suppose the one does not necessarily preclude the other.'

Gerald and I do not really hit it off, I expect that's obvious. I find much of his behaviour unsatisfactory. Welsh, I suppose.

We go along in single file. Hacking through the undergrowth.

Suddenly Douglas screams.

'Oh don't be a girl!' cries Gerald scornfully. 'It's only some old bones.'

'You must think what you will, Gerald,' I quickly interpose. 'But unless I am very mistaken, those are the rib bones of a man. And those ashes which you poke so idly with a stick, they are signs of cooking. It's as I secretly feared but didn't like to say: before long we shall have cannibals to contend with.'

Douglas snuggles against me.

Gerald stands off to one side and regards us oddly.

I have tried to tell Uncle James of my suspicions. He was sitting on a headland, gazing out to sea. I waved the rib-bone before him. He looked for a moment, but then resumed his inspection of the far horizon.

'Who would ever have imagined, William,' said my uncle, 'that this island, and so many more which abound in the broad Pacific, could have been raised by the work of little insects no bigger than a pin's head.'

'Insects, uncle?' I replied. 'Oh come now.'

Plop! A coconut fell from a tree.

'Yes, insects. Give me that piece of coral with which you are toying.'

I passed him the rib-bone.

'Do you see, William,' said my uncle after a moment, 'that on every surface there are a hundred little holes? Well in every one of these little holes once lived a sea-insect; and as these insects increase, so do the branches of the coral trees.'

'But an island, uncle?' I said.

Plop!

'The coral grows at first at the bottom of the sea,' said my uncle wearily. 'There it is not disturbed by wind or wave. By degrees it increases, advancing higher and higher towards the surface; then it is like those reefs you see out there beyond the lagoon, William. Of course it never grows above the surface of the water for if it did the tiny animals would die.'

'Then how does it become an island?'

'By very slow degrees,' said my uncle. 'And frequently the droppings of seabirds play a not inconsiderable part. But run along now William and read your Bible. My leg pains me. I promise we shall speak of this another time.'

Alas, it was not to be. Our time together on Fortunate Island had drawn nearly to an end. Indeed, Uncle James was the first of our number to be captured and eaten by cannibals.

A few days after the conversation I have just set down, Gerald, Douglas and I were out exploring. Gerald walking ahead. Douglas and I secretly holding hands.

We came down to a beautiful sandy bay. Something big, a tree stump or barrel, was rolling in the gentle surf. We ran towards it.

Sweet Jesus! It was the hideously distended leg of my uncle, James Appleby.

I realised at once that my uncle had been captured by cannibals, that these same cannibals had cooked and no doubt eaten him, yet had first removed his swollen limb as a precaution against food poisoning.

We were clearly dealing with a highly intelligent, if savage, people.

It was time to take command.

'Douglas,' I said, 'you are cool; while Gerald, you are fearless. But I am cool *and* fearless, a combination of the qualities you possess individually, and therefore I propose to be your leader, offering cool but fearless leadership. Now let us go at once and warn the others.'

Then rough hands seized me and I knew that the savages had crept up on us even as we talked.

PART THE SECOND

We have been prisoners of the cannibals for several days now. Few of us survived the initial attack; and those among us who have had the fortune (or misfortune!) to keep our lives must witness the savages swaggering past our palisaded compound, patting their bellies and saying the name 'James Appleby' in tones of gratitude and wonder. Our captors seem to be making a special point of fattening the three Appleby girls. The unfortunate young women grow visibly from day to day, probably the steady diet of breadfruit is responsible, and they anxiously inspect their figures in the dress-length mirror which Mange Tout has installed inside the compound.

The leader of the cannibal band is a big, rough man, who names himself Jules Verne, while his lieutenant, the afore-mentioned Mange Tout, is even more terrible to behold. Mange Tout claims to be the offspring of a shark and a witch, and when he smiles, the row of sharp, triangular teeth which glint along his jaw lends a terrible credence to his tale.

All the same, there is something likeable about the fellow.

I am resolved to find some way of teaching these people Christian precepts. The thing will be to win their confidence. Already a few of them gather each morning for my Bible readings, it's quite encouraging. But each night the drums begin to beat and then the terrible fires glow in the distance. The air fills with the aroma of roasting flesh.

I am deeply puzzled by the cannibals' walk. Often when a group go about together, with Jules Verne at their head, I observe that they will pause. Jules Verne will move his head from side to side and sniff the air; then he will lift his knee up almost to the chin, stepping forward in the same movement, and walk on as before. His men follow in single file, one by one making the same curious motion. It is as if they are stepping over some unseen barrier.

Each night the air fills with songs which chill the blood.

> *Strip ze skin! Quarter ze body!*
> *Skin, head, hands, feet and bowels —*
> *Set zem aside, oh set zem aside.*
> *We catch ze blood in a pannikin.*
> *We eat ze 'eart and liver first.*
> *Aha! Ho ho! Zut alors!*

We clutch one another for comfort. Douglas and I do, anyway. So do Gerald and poor Mrs Appleby. Also the two remaining Appleby girls. The eldest girl, Madge, has already been carried off to the cannibal kitchen.

Each day I am taken to visit Jules Verne in his headquarters, we talk together, we chew the fat. It is probably the fact that I have given him a jigsaw of Edinburgh Castle that makes him favour me in this way. Usually I help him find the four corners; then he sets to and makes it up during the day, destroying it again at nightfall.

Another thing that has happened is I have taught Jules and his closest advisers how to play Monopoly. They seem to have an instinctive understanding of the game. I may have forgotten to say that with all the confusion during the mutiny I managed to smuggle away a few things like that, things that would be good for trading. They have certainly come in handy.

We all make sure Jules wins, of course. By the end of a typical game, Jules owns most of London, while I have spent many rounds languishing in jail!

Strange to say, I believe I am beginning to win the respect of these rough, untutored South Sea Islanders. Gerald, always quick to offer an opinion, says that they are not South Sea Islanders at all, but French adventurers who have stayed in the Pacific so many years that they have descended to a savage condition. But this seems highly implausible.

The cannibals are certainly not Christians. They worship a mysterious creature whom they address by the name 'Zodiac'. After their evening feasting, they gather on the shores of the lagoon, a terrifying sight in the moonlight, and cry the name of their god. They make strange huffing and puffing noises, and their strange stepping motions.

Of course there is debate amongst our little party, but I am of the view that the cannibals are not entirely devoid of intelligence.

I dream of the day when these frank, unlettered creatures will bring me their idols and cry: 'Take zese zings, zese *Zodiacs*. Zey were once our gods, but now we are ashamed of zem. Take zem 'ence, for we wish zat we never more may behold zem again!'

But each night the cannibal drums beat out their messages of death. The second Appleby girl, her name slips my mind, has been taken away. And Mange Tout, when he came yesterday to clean the mirror, stared at Mrs Appleby for several minutes and said something about the annual widow-strangling ceremony.

I have taken to spying on Gerald and my aunt. Gerald is a regular rascal where a pretty girl is concerned.

They spend hours and hours together in the far corner of the compound. They believe they are unobserved.

Gerald lies on his back, and Mrs Appleby smoothes back the curly chestnut hair from his temples.

'Would you like to have me for a mama?' she asks.

'I would rather have you — for — for — '

Gerald hesitates.

'Well, dear, for what? Speak out,' says Mrs Appleby in an encouraging tone.

'I was going to say, for a sweetheart, ma'am. You are so very lovely.'

'Am I lovely?' my aunt repeats, looking at her handsome figure in the looking glass. Running the palms of her hands across her hips.

The hot blood mounts to Gerald's face and makes it burn.

'How you blush! Why do you blush so?' she says.

'I don't know, ma'am. It comes to me when I talk to you, I think. I have these stirrings in my loins.'

'Strings in your loins?' exclaims my aunt. 'Why, how very strange! But you cannot have me for a sweetheart, Gerald. I am a widow in mourning, and the aunt of your young friend, William. At all events, we shall soon be eaten by these cannibals.'

'Still, I may love you quietly and at a distance, ma'am. You cannot help people loving you.'

'You funny boy,' she exclaims. 'Come here, you funny boy.'

And soon, I am afraid, she is all over him.

I have solved the problem of the cannibals' walk. Jules Verne believes that there are deadly invisible rays stretched across the surface of the island, they are like wires drawn taut a few inches above the ground. When Jules pauses and sniffs, lifting his knee towards his chin, he is first locating, then stepping over, these treacherous obstacles.

I have all this from Mange Tout, who has begun to confide in me and is plainly sceptical of the mysterious rays. Yet he, and the rest of Jules Verne's savage band, follow their leader in every point. Occasionally one of them will trip, or pretend to trip, then fall to the ground howling. At such moments, Jules Verne laughs hideously; and all those still on their feet join in.

The cannibals take very great care in the preparation of their food. Perhaps Gerald is right after all, there is certainly a Gallic quality to that. They took away the last of the Appleby girls this morning, and Mange Tout tells me in confidence that, after she has been bled, she will be marinaded for several hours before the actual process of cooking commences.

They anoint Miranda — that is her name, Miranda — they anoint her with quassia chips and rue, with the root of tormentil and ears of barley, with slippery elm powder and the bark of wild cherry, with bladderwrack and pulp of the banyan, olibanum gum and coltsfoot, with wood betony and extract of underquil.

In the distance, the terrible drums begin again.

Each day when I am escorted to Jules Verne's headquarters to play Monopoly, I find myself pretending to step over the invisible rays. It is surprisingly easy to get into the habit. Jules Verne is most impressed by my behaviour and has explained to me that the rays are most dense around the headquarters building itself. The closer you approach, the greater the number of wires.

Near Jules Verne's hut is the impaled head of my uncle, James Appleby. He gazes out to sea through sightless eyes, as though he is scanning the horizon for a sail. A sail he knows will never come.

These cannibals do not eat the heads of their victims, they preserve them, and the procedures are really rather elaborate. Mange Tout has begun to instruct me in the treatment of heads.

We are at the Monopoly board.

'If the head is very much larger than the neck,' says Mange Tout, 'you must cut the throat lengthwise to remove the head. It is immaterial whether the eyes are taken out before the head is skinned or after.'

Jules Verne passes Go.

'The gouge,' continues Mange Tout, 'should go well to the back of the eye and separate the ligament which holds it to the socket.

Should the gouge go into the eye,' warns Mange Tout, 'it will let out the moisture, which often damages the skin. Some people,' he continues, 'crush the skull slightly to make it come out of the skin easily, but this I do not personally advise.'

Jules Verne puts a hotel on Mayfair.

'Remove the brains,' says Mange Tout, 'by taking out a piece of skull at the back as you cut off the neck. This we did in the case of your late uncle, James Appleby, and it really worked rather well. Then you must pull the eyes out of their cavity and fill up their place with wool soaked in arsenical soap. Anoint the head and neck well with arsenical soap, and place in the neck a piece of stick covered with wool, the end of which you must slip into the hole already made in the skull for extracting the brains.'

Mange Tout breaks off and grins with delight. He smiles with every muscle in his head! He has just won $10 in a Beauty Contest. Jules Verne looks somewhat put out, he is not really much of a sport.

But look — there! — how the smile grows fixed on Mange Tout's face, a rictus of despair, a rictus of defeat, and he falls, he falls suddenly across the Monopoly board, scattering all the houses and hotels of central London. A spear is embedded in his back.

The air fills with howls and eldritch screams. Another band of cannibals is attacking. Jules Verne and his men rush to join battle with the enemy, they are not afraid. But head over heels they go over their own invisible tripwires and are quickly defeated.

Cries of the slaughtered. The greedy earth drinks the blood of the dead.

It is hard to be sure what to make of this new development. Have we been rescued? And if so, who has rescued us? Or have we fallen into the hands of even more ferocious savages?

PART THE THIRD

It has been a time of pain and dark confusion, and I have lost all sense of time. I seem to be alone. Mrs Appleby was here, I think, my brief companion in captivity, but then was taken away. For a time I heard her cries at intervals. Then, after a time, nothing.

Time passes.

There has been no sign of Douglas/Meefanwee or of Gerald, perhaps they escaped, who knows, perhaps they were killed during the fighting between the rival bands of cannibals, it is as if they never existed. For the moment I must assume that they are dead — as dead as Jules Verne and his unfortunate followers.

I pass in and out of consciousness. Sometimes I think I can hear Meefanwee's voice, its ringing, bell-like laughter. Oh, it is like the sound of water running over stones! Then I ache for all that was mine and now is mine no longer, I ruefully touch my bruises. Then I begin to believe I can hear the raucous laughter of Gerald. He sounds as if he is drunk, laughing at his own jokes.

I fear I am delirious.

The other thing is that I seem to be underground — there are damp rock walls. What meagre light there is, comes from flaming torches. Ghastly shadows flicker across the walls and roof. My guess is that I am deep in the heart of the extinct volcano.

But hark! Rough voices, footsteps, cursings in a foreign tongue. The door of my cavern rasps open . . .

I am being alternately pushed and dragged, I hardly know which, through a series of dark, winding passages. On and on, I do not think I can endure much more, but then I am thrust out into a vast underground chamber. At the far end of this immense cavern are a hundred cannibal warriors, all in their battle finery, prostrate before a raised throne on which sits . . . a woman. The sight fills me with terror.

Dark of hair, dark of eye. Shoulderless dress and elaborate tattoos. But surely her features are those of a European? How strange!

And who is that who sits at her right hand, laughing and grunting, the torchlight flickering cruelly across his face? The hateful Gerald! There he sits beside the savage queen. As cool as a cucumber. Like some denizen of Hell.

'Gerald!' I cry. 'Where is Mrs Appleby?'

Gerald looks shifty.

I feel the woman's eyes on me, her gaze travels up and down my body, it is almost immodest, a woman her age, she must be nearly 50.

'Well, my young friend, you present me with an interesting problem. Shall I let you go, or shall you be my victim? Ha! Ha! Ha!'

She breaks into peals of hideous laughter.

'For pity's sake, your Highness!' I fall to my knees.

Gerald chuckles. Pleasure fairly swaggers across his features.

'William,' he says, 'may I introduce you to Mrs Llewellyn Davies.'

PART THE FOURTH

Well, how extraordinary!

We have been talking excitedly all evening. I have not been a prisoner at all, just sick with a sudden fever, probably from drinking the cannibal wine.

How strangely things have turned out! It seems that Mrs Llewellyn Davies is Gerald's old landlady. Gerald named an island after her earlier in the story. Well, she was more than his landlady, I suppose that's obvious. She ran a rooming house in Bangor, and Gerald lived there when he was doing his teacher training.

Meefanwee is not Meefanwee. I had the spelling wrong, she is Myfanwy. She is actually Mrs Llewellyn Davies' daughter. It is not clear who her father was, but it seems that Gerald is an obvious candidate, at any rate Myfanwy calls him 'Father'. Apparently when Myfanwy was a child her mother vanished, but the lonely child never believed the story about her mother being dead, and after she left high school she began to search the broad Pacific, she never gave up hope. She had adventure after adventure, of course, the Pacific is that sort of place, and one day she disguised herself as a boy, stowed away on a ship called the *Tia Maria* and, well, the rest is history . . .

The only wrong note in all this is Mrs Appleby. I am afraid that

Mrs Llewellyn Davies found out about her relationship with Gerald and at once gave her to her savage followers. They feasted on her flesh that evening. Gerald does not seem to mind.

'But how ever did Mrs Llewellyn Davies — sorry, your mother — come to be here in the first place? Queen of a cannibal island and everything?'

I am talking to Myfanwy. We are down at the beach, we have been swimming in the clear lagoon, there is one of those astonishing sunsets out beyond the reef.

'Put your hand there, William, yes there, that's it, mmm that's lovely.'

'Well?'

'Well what, William?'

'Well are you going to answer my inquiry about your mother?'

'Oh *that*! Well, William, I have not quite gathered all of the details yet, I am just so happy to have found her at last. But you will remember that years ago a Welsh rugby supporters' tour group went missing, it was after the tour itself had finished — traditional forward dominance had told against us, as everyone predicted — and they went on a Pacific Island cruise, the supporters I mean, not the team, it was part of the original package.'

I nod.

'Well, William, as you probably also know, the boat disappeared, just vanished off the face of the earth, it was in all the newspapers at the time, no one could make any sense of it. Oooh, that's so good, press a little harder, oh yes darling. Well, it seems that the cruise ship was rammed by a mysterious submarine — Russian, French, American, no one seems to know. But the ship simply broke apart. It was all over in a matter of minutes. Everyone went to the bottom.'

'Except your mother,' I interpose.

'Except my mother. You see, she had been playing deck rugby, and was fortunate enough to be holding the ball at the precise moment of collision. Mother clung to the ball for dear life, it kept her afloat, she simply clung to it, hardly knowing what she was

102

doing, till eventually she was washed up on the shores of this island, just a few yards from where we presently sit. It saved her life, you know, that rugby ball.'

'What a piece of luck! How extraordinary!'

'Yes, this is one of those cases where the truth is very much stranger than fiction.'

'But how did she come to acquire such power over these savage islanders?' I ask. 'She does not seem to be especially Christian, yet it is truly wonderful, the way in which they are obedient to her. And why did she attack Jules Verne? Had she seen you and Gerald, do you think, and set out to rescue you, or what?'

'I cannot say, William. It may simply be the volatile politics of the South Pacific. But I have not yet pursued these matters with her, so for the moment they must remain loose ends. Surely you can cope with a few loose ends, my darling? Now, would you like me to put my hand somewhere on you, what about there, shall I touch you there, does that feel good?'

I have resolved to build a raft. Myfanwy is helping me, she is sorry to see me bent on departure but she understands when I tell her I cannot have Gerald for a father-in-law, it is simply out of the question. The raft is made from the trunks of that selfsame tree whose merits were expounded, so long ago, by my late uncle, James Appleby. How little we guessed what lay in store! And even Uncle James could not have known that I would one day find a use for the coconut tree which even he had failed to anticipate!

From time to time Myfanwy and I embrace as of old, but now there is a distance. The sadness of departure lies between us.

During the day I work at building my raft. At night we join the others and listen to Mrs Llewellyn Davies read from her Visitors Book, she does a few entries each evening, the whole tribe assembles.

'The weather exceeded only by the company' — Littleford family, Birmingham.
'Vielen Dank!' — Familie G. Prutz, Hamburg.

'Thank you, very nice' — Jim and Noeline Carter, Tasmania.

The cannibals think it is a sacred book. After each entry they gasp and applaud. They show their appreciation in the usual manner.

I look out at the lagoon, at the clouds of spray above the reef, seabirds diving and calling . . . and beyond lies all the vastness of the blue Pacific!

My raft is ready, it is time to go.

I shall be adrift for days, maybe for weeks. But eventually some ship will spot my ragged sail, heave to and take me aboard, faint and delirious from the pitiless sun, full of a wild story, cannibals and a mutiny, poor fellow, look! is that a Bible he is clutching, take him below . . .

I gaze on Myfanwy, my companion in so many trials. I take her photograph. I touch her lips, her hair, her perfect breasts. Then I turn to go. That is how it is, adventure and regret, there is no getting away from it, we live in the broad Pacific, meeting and parting shake us, meeting and parting shake us, it is always touch and go.

NONCHALANCE
OR
THE NEW LAND: A PICTURE BOOK

1. *The bishops*

THE BISHOPS COME ashore. Tell me, they say, what is the name of this country? Does everyone here speak English or is it just the one or two of you? Please understand that we shall need hotel accommodation only until we have made somewhat more permanent arrangements. Be particularly careful with the blue suitcases, they contain flutes and ammunition. And here, sailing up the harbour, is the ship which brings the soldiers' wives.

2.

The wives come ashore. Here are the wives in the museum, their first real expedition from the hotel. What is this brown thing? asks one. Does it do something important? Can we take photographs in here or must we buy the postcards? In that case where is the *bureau de change*, the *cambio*, the *wechsel*?

And here is violent death, the brown thing. Here is sunset in the park, the first light of dawn, the flag flapping. The soldiers' wives are wondering about the harbour-lights tour. They have been told that the harbour-lights tour is excellent value for money, but they have only recently arrived and they want to sit down for a bit and think about it properly.

3. *Getting off to a good start*

The first step is to approach local inhabitants as if you are their guest. Move slowly. If possible, acquire a few words of local greeting and repeat them to everyone you meet. Hold out your hand to those you meet in a gesture that includes them in your experience. If you are male, be circumspect in your dealings with the local womenfolk. If you are female and alone, be glad that you are you, on the move and pleasing yourself most of the time.

4. *Making the characters come alive as individuals*

This can be done in a number of ways, but many new authors imagine it is all done by giving a description of clothing, whereas this doesn't really help. Picture a group of soldiers, all dressed in exactly similar clothing, and think of what makes each one an individual. How could you describe one of them in order to distinguish him from his fellows?

It can't be done by describing the clothing, so something else has to be considered. Well, one man might have, say, a ginger moustache, another may have huge hands, a third may walk as though expecting to fall down a flight of steps at the very next stride.

5. *The soldiers*

The soldiers are all at the front, from which word rarely gets back. Occasionally a private note to a loved one is intercepted and sold on the streets by enterprising youngsters. But most visitors are too embarrassed to purchase them; local residents do not usually have the money.

6.

Here is a photograph of the first flag, which was run up on the first sewing machine, which should be in the museum but has not survived. A soldier gazes up towards the flag, his face alight with expectation. And here is a photograph of the boat with its cargo of bishops looking disappointed (a) at the tiny jetty and (b) at the rather sparse welcoming party. Tell me, they say, what is the name of this country? Do you always have such beautiful weather?

7. *Giving and getting*

Not all of your contact with local people will involve getting something from them. Don't forget that you have a unique opportunity to bring them something from your own culture. Go ahead and show them what it looks like: try postcards, or magazines. If you have a camera, let the local people, especially the children, look through the viewfinder. Put on a telephoto so they can get a new look at their own countryside. Take along an instant print camera, photograph them and give them the ensuing print. Most important: *become involved.* Carry aspirins to cure headaches, real or imagined. If someone seems to need help, why not lend a hand? Contribute yourself as an expression of your culture.

8. *Another thing*

Another thing. On some of the more travelled routes the local children, used to being given sweets by passing soldiers, will swarm around, their sticky hands held out for more. The best course is to smile (always) and refuse them. Show them pictures, your favourite juggling act or a noble piece of stone (e.g. Edinburgh Castle). Then give them something creative, like pencils.

9. *The sadness competition*

The soldiers' wives are enjoying a night out. They have a block booking at the monthly sadness competition. Of course, they are only spectators, crammed into the back stalls, although as one of them (Irene) says to another (Trudy), sometimes the way you end up feeling, you might just as well be up there with the sailors as sitting down here watching. Trudy pulls a face, entering into the spirit of things.

The entrants are all sailors, far from home. The rules require contestants to think of something sad, so that the feeling will visibly transform their faces. As well, they must supply the saddest word they know and repeat it several times. The best words tend to be those like 'nonchalance', for they are filled with the sadness of seeming more sophisticated than the states of mind to which they refer. Many contestants concentrate their thoughts upon the ordinary sadness of the past — the oceans crossed, the lands and cities never to be regained, the families and sweethearts left behind, a single half-remembered cadence . . . tra la. Others prefer to think about the future, the emptiness of everything to come.

Tonight's winner is a young sailor. It turns out that he has been thinking of his present circumstances, which he defines in a word: 'unlimitless'. After his victory walk, he is bound hand and foot and taken away. He will go forward to the next round.

(All the same, said Trudy, I think I will just go on back to the hotel if that is all right with the rest of you. This has been quite enough excitement for me for one night! But aren't things getting off to a wonderful start!)

10. *A letter from the front*

My dear Irene,

What a snug little place this is! After a hard day of manoeuvres, a quiet smoke and a read in such comfortable surroundings are indeed something to look forward to. But how much more delightful this spot would be if it were your home as well as mine! Let us hope this dream will be fulfilled at no very distant date!

Could you have seen how eagerly I tore open your letter you would have felt well repaid for your trouble in writing it. What delightful things it contains, I can hardly bring myself to believe that it is I to whom all the sweet and tender things are said!

My darling, your sweet letter makes it very hard for me to curb my impatience until the day when we shall be together always. I wonder if you too sit and muse over our future home. Have you planned it just as you want it? Somehow I feel you have, and I, too, seem to know just what those plans are, for our tastes and ideas are so similar that were you to arrange every detail of our house, I'm sure I should not have a single alteration to suggest. Write again soon, my darling, for your letters charm away the pain and weariness of this ghastly war.

Your loving
'Ginger'

11. *First things first*

The first Highland Pipe Band. The first Amateur Weightlifting Association. The first affiliated branch of Alcoholics Anonymous. The first Shipwreck Relief Society. The first Mission to Seamen. The first Coopworth Sheep Society. The first Association of Teachers of Speech and Drama. The first one-armed bandit. The first alcoholic.

The first honeymoon hotel. The first Returned Services Association. The first accountant. The first tourist hotel with full en suite facilities. The first Santa Gertrudis Breeders Society. The first Association of Beauty Therapists. The first Australian Ambassador. The first Soviet Ambassador. The first baby. The first newspaper, with a photograph of the first baby. The first Licensing Trust. The first New Zealand Ambassador. The first cuckoo.

12. *First things first (continued)*

The first school which the first baby will attend. The first Minister of Education. The first Volunteer Fire Brigade. The first American Ambassador. The first employed person. The first unemployed person. The first turning on the right. The first turning on the left. The first public lending library. The first massage parlour. The first overdue book. The first State lottery. The first free elections. The first death from natural causes. The first headstone. The first Esperanto meeting. The first campaign to lower the drinking age. The first film society. The first chamber music concert. The first street riots. The first Alfa Romeo Owners' Club. The second New Zealand Ambassador. The first

109

Guild of Agricultural Journalists. The first dealer gallery. The first light of dawn.

13. *Dealing with deserters, individual prisoners, spies, negotiators, contingents of prisoners*

Take off your shoes. Empty your pockets. Cut the lining of your coat open. The lining of your hat. Have you any letters or other papers on you? Give me your memorandum book. What branches of the service? Are the troops well clothed, well cared for, and in good spirits? Are you here to negotiate? Who sent you? What do you want? Follow me. If you show yourselves willing and obedient, you have nothing to fear. Right (left) turn! March! Halt!

Are you hungry? Are you cold? Do you possess your own bishopric? Is it nearby? Can we journey there on foot? On the other side of the ranges? Beyond the seas? Please write your answer on this sheet of paper which I have brought with me expressly for the purpose. The ambulance will fetch you very soon. Remain quietly in a lying position. Sleep soundly. I will stay with you. Tomorrow we will make a start on expressions pertaining to conduct.

14. *The first short story*

'I was lying on the hillside in the sun, minding my own business as you might say, just soaking up the unfamiliar sunshine and wondering vaguely about the details of my life. My flute lay beside me. My shovel lay beside me. I was resting after my labours. Suddenly I was aware that men with guns were gathered round about me, one of their number crying loud above the chatter of the rest, "Are you the dying man?" '

15. *A letter from the front*

Dear Trudy,
It is useless for me to pretend that your letter was not a great blow, but at the same time I must confess that I had a feeling that your answer would be 'No'. At the moment I

feel as though I shall not be able to stand it, for you are very, very dear to me, but I shall try to put the best complexion on the matter and bear my grief like a man.

It will, I think, be better for both of us if we do not see each other again for some little time, after which I hope we shall be able to meet again as really good friends. I would fight no longer in this ghastly war if I did not believe in some sort of future — for all of us. Your happiness means so much to me that, if I know you are happy, I am sure I shall, in time, come to look upon the world as a place not quite so lonesome and cold as it seems at this moment.

Always your sincere friend,
'Ginger'

16. *Plots to avoid*

(a) Plots with a sex motif.
(b) Where religion plays a dominating role.
(c) Plots where sadism or brutality appear.
(d) Plots with a basis of divorce.
(e) Plots where illness or disease must be emphasised.
(f) Plots dealing with harrowing experiences of children.
(g) Plots dealing with politics.
(h) Plots where a criminal succeeds in escaping justice.
(i) Plots that just don't go anywhere, e.g. 'The king died and then the queen went to the pictures.'

17. *Characters to avoid*

(a) Those with impediments of speech.
(b) Those with ugly physical infirmities.
(c) Idiots or those mentally afflicted.

There are exceptions to this of course, but for the beginner, the rule should be, avoid these types of people.

18. *Photographs*

The procession of coaches winds up the hill. Yo-ho-ho. The sailors are playing their flutes and drinking hard liquor, doing the things that come naturally to hard seafaring men. Each year, at this time, they make this expedition. They bring with them their photographs, captured images of bodies of water they have crossed: the Andaman Sea, the Tasman, the Yellow and Red Seas, the Ross Sea, the Sea of Okhotsk, the Java Sea.

Now they are digging holes in the green hillside, below the ancient fortifications. Custom requires one hole for every photograph. The coach drivers, bored, lean against their vehicles, rolling cigarettes. They have seen this sort of thing before. After the sailors have buried their photographs of water (the Andaman Sea, the Tasman, the Yellow and Red Seas, the Ross Sea, the Sea of Okhotsk, the Java Sea), they will eat their cut lunches, climb aboard the coaches and head on back to town.

19. *Don't forget to communicate*

This terrible lack of communication that arises many times in the work of new writers has already been dealt with to some extent. You, the author, conjure a vivid series of scenes in your mind and, satisfied yourself, fail to put down the transitional links that make the tale fully comprehensible to a stranger reading it.

You, the author, know that your female character has now left the museum and struck up a conversation with a young sailor who speaks one of the minor languages of sadness. But the reader cannot read your mind — the reader can only read what you have put on paper, which may not be enough.

And don't forget to foreshadow. If one of your characters is going to make use of a gun, then let the reader know well beforehand that a gun exists. Bang!

20. *Hope for the future*

But look at this, it is the first baby. The first newspaper, with a photograph of the first baby. This is good news to be able to carry on the first day after the dummy runs! The news from the front is sparse and is tucked away on the inside back page. The comics page is relatively unsophisticated. The correspondence column carries (1) a message from the bishops, expressing pleasure at the generous response to the first street appeal; (2) a letter about rising unemployment; (3) a request for pen-pals from Japan. There are only a few classified advertisements, but at least it is a start. The comics page is relatively unsophisticated. The whole thing probably needs a crossword or a few more photographs. A picture of one of those beauty spots where the trees come right down to the water: that would do.

21. *The black bird of my heart*

A sailor is singing. He has laid aside his flute and he sings in a voice that may or may not be carried out to sea. It depends on the wind, on the time of day, on the circumstances. He is young, the sailor, he is nonchalant, and the song he sings was popular in the fifties, before he was born. As he walks along, sauntering inland, he looks as though he expects to fall down a flight of steps at the very next stride. An older sailor taught him the song, warning him that some of the words might well be misremembered.

My tears have washed 'I love you' from . . . tra la.

But after all, it is only a song like any other. The form is fine but we will not guarantee the content. It deals with clouds and manacles, cameras and repressive legislation, martial law and inner torment. It deals with the world as we know it, at the point where it is only half imagined. Were we to ask the sailor, of course, he would disagree. He believes it is a song about his sweetheart, about whom he is not really thinking; while the children, who have begun to crowd around him holding out their sticky hands for sweets, believe it to be otherwise again: a song about the next new land, the one which is travelling by word of mouth from a place beyond the ranges, which is as yet beyond reproach, still at the stage of making up its mind.